Meter-Wide Button

Stories

Lillian Paige Walton

Sapp Press, 2020

Advanced Reading Copy

Sapp001
ISBN: 978-1-7359831-0-3

Cover art © Lillian Paige Walton,
The Writer, 2020
graphite on paper
19 in x 12.5 in

Manufactured in the United States of America

Design and typesetting by Josh Abramovici

Sapp Press, New York, NY.
368 Broadway, #506, New York, NY.
www.sapppress.com

Table of Contents

For K — to read in the bath

The Room in Which I Write

Before we continue, there is something about me that I would like you to know. You may feel so far that you have a sense of who I am. In truth, there is a lot that you don't know about me and even less that I am willing to share. For example, you do not know the reason(s) why I chose to wear the shirt I am currently wearing over any other I could have worn today. This is something that you would never know unless I were to tell you. Perhaps you thought that I had chosen this puffed-sleeve shirt because you thought I wanted to look flirty as I present this work to you. How assumptive and bizarre of you.

I am wearing this shirt because of the small rash located at the outer corner of my inner armpit. Contrary to other styles of sleeves, the puffed sleeve is engineered to avoid the armpit area and sometimes the shoulder, depending on the puff's circumference-to-arm ratio. My rash can breathe comfortably in this shirt (which I would argue is actually a blouse) without the stress of friction, which could further aggravate my condition.

Now that I have proven that you know nothing about me whatsoever, I will provide you something I would like you to know. It is important to me that you understand neither me nor my minor skin ailments, but where my work is coming from. My work is coming from the room in which I write.

The room in which I write has no door, so it must be entered from below. I enter with my head first, removing the small window of film that separates the room in which I write from the room in which I do not write. Next comes my hand, bearing a candle, as there are no lamps. There is no furniture and decor is scant, apart from a small 16th century urn that sits on a shelf high above the floor. The light from my candle cannot reach it, so I cannot be sure of its exact location. I avoid drastic movements such as jumping or coughing.

On good nights I am left alone. On bad nights snakes pass over my ankles. They are attracted to the sound of my swishing pen. Sometimes the floor is covered in water, but more often it is filled with sand. Once there was a man who held a flashlight above me as I worked. Today, he was replaced by his brother who sneezed and complained. I am spending less and less time in the room. My work has become very short. Tomorrow, I'll leave as soon as I arrive. My exit is similar to how I enter; feet first, instead of head.

Excavation

The silver instruments jingled inside of their translucent, green pouch as the young dentist lifted them off of the wheeled cart beside him. As he struggled to open the sterile seal, he glanced over at the patient sitting in the chair. Sleek, dark hair grazed the tops of her summer shoulders. Her chart stated that she was twenty five years old and allergic to shellfish. He had just read her name aloud, but had trouble calling it to mind. She was looking out of the window beside her, presumably at the excavation site below, or the waterfront just beyond it.

The dentist had come to ignore the daily noise of the archaeologists, who screamed Romance languages at each other over the sounds of their machinery. Any day now, the dentist feared, an artifact would be found and the archaeologists would be able to expand their site. It was only a matter of time before his practice would be forced to relocate. He thought of the black-and-white poster hanging in the waiting room down the hallway. It was an aerial photograph of a stone assemblage that some early humans had arranged in a ring. He liked it because he thought it looked like a grinning mouth.

The photograph had been hanging there since he had opened his practice. At the time, he couldn't afford waiting chairs, but he thought it was important for his patients to have something to look at. He glanced back at the patient. Her left foot was rocking slowly side to side; her hands were knitted together in her lap.

A mild astringent scent filled the room as the seal of the pouch was finally opened. The fragrance aroused the patient's interest. She caught the dentist entranced by something on the floor. The patient craned her neck to figure out what the dentist was seeing, but could see nothing aside from the patterned carpet, flecked with the unsavory, muted greens typical of office decor.

The dentist felt the patient's gaze and pulled himself out of his reverie. Devoid of expression, her face unnerved him. He attempted to smile at her, but the dry corners of his mouth refused to move, resulting in a grimace. The patient did not return the gesture. The dentist stretched his latex fingers open and closed around his palms and returned to his tools.

With a mechanical click, the dentist lowered the patient's chair. A tired exhale escaped through his nose as he straightened the protective bib hanging from her neck. The overhead lamp beamed down on his head. From the perspective of the patient, the light was a microscope stage upon which the outline of the dentist's hair was a shadowy amoeba. The dentist's mouth opened slightly to reveal a sizable gap between his two front teeth. He noticed the patient's wandering gaze and quickly closed his lips. He hurriedly pulled the mask that was hanging around his neck back over his ears and onto his face.

The cluster of stray curls that hung off of his forehead trembled as he adjusted his seat and leaned over the patient. The dentist paused, tool in hand. The patient's bottom lip was cracked, and the corners of her mouth were red and raw. He looked at the tray beside him, where the Vaseline was typically kept. It was gone.

His hand slipped automatically into the pocket of his trousers and around his tube of chapstick. He heard a jingle behind him as he bumped into the table.

The small pot of Vaseline had fallen on the floor, underneath the patient's chair. He let go of the balm between his fingers and reached underneath the chair to retrieve the pot.

He quickly smoothed the Vaseline onto the patient's lips, finding himself suddenly annoyed that she had brought herself to his office in such a condition. He tapped her bottom lip to encourage her to open her mouth, not realizing that he was opening his own behind his mask in the process.

The patient's mouth opened with a loud pop, like a champagne bottle being opened into a cloth. The dentist's eyes disappeared into his face as he broke into a laugh.

He grabbed the periodontal probe and mirror and began to count her teeth, noting the presence of a baby tooth on the left side of her bottom row. He consulted her chart for any mention of hypodontia, but saw nothing. He consulted the map of the patient's teeth, a fax from her previous office. A small note was scrawled beside the baby tooth on the right side of the patient's mouth. He squinted at the handwriting, puzzled by the presence of the note. He couldn't decipher it.

He returned to the patient's mouth and shifted the probe and mirror to the left side. In between the molars was a dark blue object. He tilted the mirror to get a better view. He'd thought at first that the object was a piece of candy, but it was shaped and rooted just like a tooth. He touched the tooth with the probe and felt it lock into place. Terrified, he attempted to move the tool out of her mouth. He held the patient's jaw with his left hand. The tooth resisted slightly and finally gave way. The dentist cried out. The small blue tooth was stuck to the end of the probe.

The patient gazed calmly at the dentist, unalarmed by the sight of the strange tooth. She coughed and a solid projectile shot out of her throat, whipping past the dentist's shoulder and across the room. A glass cabinet chimed as the object hit its surface then fell to the floor. The dentist stood up from the chair, walked over to where it had fallen, and found himself staring at a small silver object, covered in spittle. He could feel the patient watching him, her foot still moving side to side.

The dentist crossed the room and sat back down in the chair before the patient. His hands were trembling. He stared at the tray where the probe lay—strange tooth still attached—and began to weep.

In the lot below, a voice cried out in French. Something had been found.

Residency

One

Louise had been reading her work at under-attended events in local bookstores for nearly three years before her first short story ever made it into print. "Lizards and Lemons" was included in the December print issue of an obscure journal based in Winnipeg that prided itself on its "specific" readership. Though the story was advertised by the journal as Louise's debut, it was the twenty fourth work of serious fiction she had ever written. Due to rapidly declining sales and subscriptions following the publication, the journal switched over to becoming an exclusively online platform. Fortunately, one of the twelve print issues that were sold fell into the hands of an editor for a moderately better-known magazine. The editor showed Louise's story to a friend who was a publisher at a small independent press. The publisher enthusiastically contacted Louise about including some of her work in a short collection of contemporary American fiction.

The taste of success was sufficient enough to prompt Louise to leave her day job of six years to begin what her sister lovingly referred to as her "self-imposed residency." The money that she had squirreled away over the past decade was enough so that she could live and maintain her gym membership for at least six months, during which she would attempt to write her first novel.

On her last day at work, a small party was held for Louise in the coworking space that her company rented. A dominant office personality played music from his phone and sipped aggressively from a plastic cup. He would never venture out of a four-foot radius from the device for the remainder of the party. The others chatted nervously and picked at unsalted pretzels and deviled eggs, and got drunk on beer from unbranded cans supplied by the coworking organization. The evening's timeline, meticulously crafted by someone in HR, included a "gentle" roast at the end of the evening.

The roast was ill-fated from the start, as Louise had kept mostly to herself and did not have friends at work. Many of Louise's coworkers didn't know who she was until her departure had been announced, so it should have come as no surprise that nobody had prepared material.

The room marinated in an awkward silence until Kebin from Finance mentioned that he knew that Louise was single because she kept a framed photograph of her dead cat at her desk. There was scattered, nervous laughter and the music was quickly switched back on.

Kebin was quietly dismissed from the party and suspended from the office until he completed a mandatory online empathy training at the request of his supervisor. This went on entirely unbeknownst to Louise, who was busy carving the remaining hummus from the fiestaware bowl and contemplating prospective titles for her debut novel.

Louise awoke the next morning to a mild hangover in her studio apartment. She rose from bed and walked a few feet to the kitchen to make a cup of coffee. As the kettle boiled she drank five full glasses of water in quick succession. She returned to bed with her laptop. Louise sat with the screen of the warm device resting against her knees and opened a new file in WordBeater. As the cursor pulsed on the blank page, the panic rose within her. It was as though the anchor attaching the bed to the rest of the room had been lifted. She was floating freely and without a known destination. It was only nine in the morning and already the day felt endless. She might as well vacuum first.

Two

The initial panic and guilt subsided as Louise began to develop a routine. With no boss and no agent, Louise found that the only way to prevent herself from feeling adrift was to adhere to a strict schedule. For Louise, this meant rising at six each morning to go to the gym down the street. After working out, she would shower at the gym, get dressed, and grab a palm-sized piece of fruit (as unblemished and spherical as she could find) from the market stand and head home. Taking into account the possible complications that might interfere with her ability to get home in a timely manner—such as sidewalk construction or the man that lingered outside the bakery every morning and offered her ten dollars to see her breasts—the timeline Louise had meticulously crafted for herself had her back at her doorstep at 8:00 a.m. sharp. She was seated at her writing desk by 8:04 a.m., where she would—with the exception of noon lunch—work straight until six in the evening, save for Fridays, in which she permitted herself an early leave of 3:00 p.m. In the evenings she tidied and vacuumed for thirty minutes. On weekends she bought groceries and avoided the bakery.

The book began to take shape as did her home office. She purchased a large piece of butcher paper and drew an eight-foot-tall fiddle leaf fig tree with big green leaves and a simple white porcelain drainage pot beneath it. She tacked the drawing up on the wall beside the window. The apartment was kept frigid—a constant sixty degrees fahrenheit at all times. Words flowed from her fingertips.

Returning each morning from the gym, Louise entered her apartment and closed the door behind her. As she stood surveying the room, she felt two things: one was the slimy core of eaten fruit in her hand, and the other, a sense of divine satisfaction. It was a similar sort of satisfaction that might be experienced by one who also greatly enjoys hand-addressing letters or a person who, after experimenting with various furniture arrangements, finally feels at peace with their home decor. Both examples described Louise. The studio apartment felt sacred with its high ceilings and library-like silence. The air conditioning unit—a staple of the home office—hummed softly from the window sill on the far side of the room.

After locking and bolting the door behind her, Louise opened the large wooden chest to the left of the front door and pulled long sheets of tarp from it. A month ago she'd stumbled across a forum for freelancers on how to create a productive work environment at home. Username *FocuseDrick1201* emphasized the importance of minimalism, commenting that to obscure a distraction from view was to remove it from thought "or, to use a cliché, 'out of sight, out of mind.'" The phrase became Louise's inner mantra as she began her circumambulation around the writing desk, covering her bed, sofa, television and all other threatening pieces of furniture with the blue tarp. The bookshelf, spanning floor to ceiling with an impressive collection of reference materials, of course, was spared.

As she sat down at her writing desk, Louise truly felt as though she were at the center of a machine, or the heart of the organism. The chair crinkled as she adjusted herself. The cushion, in need of reupholstering, had not been spared in the preparation of the room. She opened her laptop and stared at the twenty-one page manuscript. Deciding that she needed a warm up, she opened the drawer on the right side of the desk, producing a leather-bound notebook. She reached for her prized fountain pen, nestled in its corresponding case.

At eleven o'clock Louise's watch clucked with a soft reminder that it was time to prepare her second cup of tea. She paused on the way to the kitchenette, noting an unusual sound coming from the air conditioning unit. The machine was a foreign entity, but had suddenly become more human in its expression of difficulty. Louise often pitied it, how it worked ceaselessly to keep her cool as its own backside was exposed to the sweltering August heat. The poor thing had no vacation during the summer months, when

Louise kept it running even while she was out. Louise simply couldn't bear to be warm, not even at night; she would curl up to watch cop dramas in her bed, preferring to shiver beneath the covers. At times, she felt uneasy in the unit's presence, feeling it stare back at her, its vented grill shaped like a grimace.

Through the glass windowpane, she looked over the unit onto the visible street below. A shirtless man was rummaging through a neighbor's compost bin. No clouds cast shadows or flicked light on and off of the pavement. Pure, relentless solar radiation baked the concrete.

Louise opened her glassware cabinet to reveal several rows of identical glasses, organized by color and pattern. She took a striped glass and used a small tapside attachment to fill her glass three quarters of the way full with purified water. She paused and, with her nose scrunched into a position of disgust, picked a microscopic particle off of the side of the tap before turning it off. She glanced at her watch. Outside, it was currently ninety six degrees Fahrenheit.

Louise walked over to the air conditioning unit again. She wondered if the temperature inside the room had increased and waved her hand over the vent to check for cool air.

The man was still at the compost bin, leaning so far over it that it looked as though he might fall in. His spine was visible through the skin and revealed an extreme s-shaped curve on his back. Beads of his sweat glinted in the sun. In a strange deviation from her typical routine, she returned to her desk without taking a snack or making lunch.

Three

Louise stopped herself from reading the manuscript, alarmed by the sound that was coming from the opposite end of the room. She jumped. The air conditioning unit was emitting thick clouds of smoke. She imagined the machine bursting into flames, or worse—splintering into a thousand shards that would fly across the room, destroy her laptop, and ricochet into her eyes.

The machine stopped. Louise sat frozen as an unfamiliar silence settled in the room. Traffic whirred from a distant highway, a woman spoke loudly on the phone somewhere in the street below, cans and bottles clinked—likely the sounds of the man still searching through more bins. Louise began to panic and walked over to the air conditioning unit. Its once-pristine vent was charred black.

She grabbed the power cord and tried unplugging and plugging the appliance in again to no effect. She downloaded a troubleshooting manual on her watch. Following the instructions, she felt the sides of the machine and examined the electrical cable for any irregularities. The Common Issues section had no examples that remotely resembled her current situation. Nowhere was there a reference to a smoking device, a charred vent. Louise phoned tech support and waited on hold for nine minutes and thirteen seconds before her call was answered. They could send someone to take a look at the unit free of charge because the item was still under warranty. The earliest they could come by was between 5:30 and 7:00pm.

Louise tapped her pen nervously on the counter. What if someone with an appointment dropped out and had to cancel, she asked, could they come sooner?

The man replied that it was possible but doubtful. It had been a hell of a busy summer and there were five remaining refrigerator repairs to be completed before they closed for the evening. You see, he said, these things don't fix themselves.

Louise replied that the matter was urgent, as she worked from home.

The man apologized and suggested she try going to a coffee shop or a friend's home until the repair could be done. His remark was followed by such silence on the other end that he was not sure if she was still on the line.

Finally, Louise emerged, quietly muttering something about having been a faithful buyer of appliances from the company for nearly a decade. She agreed to the appointment, then hung up.

It was difficult to tell if the room had grown warmer or if Louise had become heated by the upset. She touched the back of her neck, damp with sweat. The room smelled like hot plastic. She stared at the blind-less, drapeless window. The apartment would grow hotter as the sun grew stronger throughout the afternoon. The watch reflected a similar prediction, showing increasing temperatures until 6:00 p.m.. Louise returned to the desk at the center of the room, spending a few minutes on her watch looking for the settings to control the ceiling fan. She set the fan on a medium-high speed by moving the black dot across a line with her thumb. She jumped as the stacks of paper on her desk fluttered then planted a tape dispenser on top of them to keep them from flying away. Once the paper was secure, she settled back into the chair.

Four

Her button-down blouse was soaked at the back and the pits. A small pool of sweat had collected between her breasts, seeping into the band of her camisole. Her linen viscose-blend skirt clung to the back of her thighs. She looked at her watch. The fan, at maximum oscillation speed, rocked precariously over the desk.

Louise shielded her eyes as she turned toward the window. It was as though the sun had lowered itself down from the sky to peek its flaming head into the room. She couldn't recall it ever getting so bright.

Louise's landlord, a Croatian woman in her eighties, lived on the first floor of the building. Even in August, the woman had her windows open. Windows open to noise, open to the smell of garbage, open to wet, stagnant city air. Only the quiet ceiling fan wicked overhead. The woman would rise to collect Louise's rent check, uttering a small "Thank you, Lowis." Black hair was plastered to her forehead and there was a line of sweat beneath her breasts. She never seemed to be the least uncomfortable.

Louise stood at the window. The electrical cord for the AC unit dangled above the outlet. In one last attempt for salvation she tried plugging it in again. Nothing happened. She hated the idea of removing the barrier between the outside world and her own, inviting in the pollution, the noise, the smell and all other uncontrollables and distractables. The apartment reeked of hot plastic. The tarp was baking under the heat of the sun. The area rug, the desk, the upholstered chair announced their material compositions, each releasing its own unique stink into the air. Louise squinted out the window. The man who had been rummaging through the bin was gone. A shadow of clothes on a clothesline jittered on the pavement. She heaved the window open and grasped the dead appliance tightly in her hands. She took a deep breath to prepare to lift it. *One, Two, Three...*

Five

The fountain pen hit the floor, cracking open at the base. She had flinched too hard as a car drove by. It sounded as though it were right behind her.

Six

A cluster of tiny, frustrated marks appeared in the upper lefthand corner of Louise's notebook. She sat hunched before her computer screen like a grotesque on a cathedral ledge. She was in the middle of page thirty-four, suddenly aware that she could not recall anything since page thirty-one. Reading the words conjured no mental image of their meaning, a dilemma which reminded her of trying to read a menu when she had gone too long without eating. She hadn't eaten anything but the piece of fruit that morning. She blamed the traffic, she blamed the man that was no longer there, she blamed the neighbors for leaving their compost bin in such a vulnerable area. She blamed the neighbors in her apartment building and their children, whose footsteps she could suddenly hear in the hall as they returned from their day camps. There was sweat between her breasts, damp at her back, collecting in the pockets of skin behind her knees. It was in her ears. She dabbed at them with the corner of her blouse.

Remembering something, she rose from the chair and crunched across the floor to the far end of the room. She lifted a piece of tarp to expose a set of wooden drawers. A small drawer on the top left was full of autographed ticket stubs from various operas. She fished around inside the next drawer, her watch clacking against the wood interior. Victory. Her hand emerged from the drawer, producing a small plastic case. Two custom-fitted earplugs rattled inside like weird beans. She stuck them in her ears and waddled back to the desk. She looked at the screen, reviewing her progress:

> *All his life, Cramp had been waiting for a romance just like this. Perhaps it had always been there, waiting for him as he passed it by on his way to the bookstore or something. He was uncovering new things about himself each day, for which he considered himself to be truly lucky. As a young*

man, he'd always thought that he was only into big boobs, but as he grew older, he realized he was also kind of into small and medium-sized boobs, too.

A droplet of Louise's sweat fell onto the keyboard. She wiped it away anxiously. She looked down at her clothes, a Rorschach blot of sweat across her skirt, her shirt. Her cardigan sweater lay in a wet pile beside the desk. The tenets of structure were collapsing around her. She imagined the desk chair as a small row boat. She sat in the boat in the middle of the sea, drifting away, looking over her shoulder to see the collapsed ruins of her apartment-temple behind her. A cracked laptop screen glinting among collapsed plinths and columns. A cloud of smoke billowing atop the destruction. The fires burning blue on account of the tarp.

It seemed ridiculous to continue to suffer, to ruin her clothes, which were mostly dry clean only. If she took them off, nobody would see her. She had to push on. The man on the phone had told her that the repair person would call when they were on the way. It could be any moment now. She pulled the wet shirt off of her head and let it fall with a slap to the floor. It was remarkable how heavy the simple cotton knit sounded. She stood and unzipped her skirt, letting it fall to the floor with a similar slap. She left them exactly as they had fallen. Out of laziness or dignity, she left her camisole and underwear on. She stared at the laptop screen, seeing only grey lines on a white page. She squinted at the line again and began to write.

Miranda's green eyes shone as she blinked the tears out of her eyes. Cramp didn't really know what to say to her, but wanted to express his desire to see her again.

"I will definitely text u," he said, smoothing the fabric of her dress over her tight backside. "Maybe not tonight, but soon tho." The armored car rolled up beside them and Cramp got in. He flashed her a peace sign from the window. Miranda's dress rippled in the wind as she waved back to him. Her shoes were cool.

The ear plug slipped out of Louise's left ear and fell to the floor with a soft pat. As she leaned over to pick it up, the right ear plug popped out. Louise paused, wet earplugs in hand, as she listened to the noise coming from the apartment above, the soft moans of her neighbors having sex. At times, it sounded as though they were taking a break to drag something heavy across the floor. A third person was perhaps involved. Everything sounded so close. Paper thin. If she flicked the ceiling, they would fly into the air. But alas, they were flicking each other while she was stuck below, waiting for relief from the repair person.

The neighbor moaned. Louise closed the laptop shut. Enough was enough. She rose from her chair and moved toward the front door, unbolting and unlocking it with a series of quick and aggressive movements. She paused, noticing a small patch of eczema on her forearm, and remembered she wasn't wearing clothes. The old door knob came off the door as she let go of it. It rolled across the floor.

Louise walked back into the center of the room, absentmindedly tracing the patch of dry skin with her finger. Abandoned glasses of water were littered across the desk and floor. The tarp was pulled back to expose distractables, the drawer still hanging ajar at the far end of the room. Oddly, she felt unmoved to fix or adjust any of it. She felt heavy. Perhaps it was her underwear and camisole, soaked with the water she had lost. She looked at the laptop screen unhappily. She had lost a lot. The fan was working overtime, lurching back and forth as though it, too, were being fucked.

Seven

In truth, she couldn't remember the last time she'd had anyone over.

Eight

A long rectangle of golden light fell across the room as the sun set gradually in the sky. The upstairs neighbors had fallen quiet, but now the downstairs neighbors moaned below. Cans and bottles resumed clinking outside the window. Someone screamed in the streets, searching for a lost pet. Louise stood precariously on the window sill, notebook clenched between her teeth. She held onto the trim to steady herself as she squinted into the golden light coming through the glass. A tape dispenser was wedged into the front or her camisole, between her sweaty breasts. She transferred the notebook from between her teeth into her hand. She tore the pages off the spiral spine and taped them to the glass. The notebook travelled back and forth between her hands and mouth as she worked.

A bird landed on the window ledge. Louise felt its soft landing through the screen. It remained as she continued, the golden rectangle of light growing smaller as she covered the window pane with paper. Soon, she was out of blank notebook pages. The bird stirred as Louise flipped through the notebook, hesitating over her notes. At this point, she could not turn back. The notes ripped just as easily off of the spiral spine as the blank pages had. This in itself felt like a sign that things were finally coming together as they should. Carefully, Louise lowered herself down to admire her work. The notes had left the notebook, but were still with her. They glowed from behind like stained glass.

Her eyes shifted between the small clock in the right hand corner of the screen and her wrist watch. Her stomach growled. It was 8:00 p.m., a half hour after her estimated appointment window and she still hadn't received a call from the repair company. The screen of the computer went dark. Louise pressed a key to awaken the device from sleep mode. No response. She uncoiled the charger to the left of the drawer and plugged it in. No light, no response. The device was hot to the touch. She took the glass of water from the desk and poured it slowly down her front.

As the sun dipped into the horizon, something left Louise. It came from a place below her ribs and caused the bird to flit suddenly from the ledge of the window.

Nine

After completing his mandatory empathy training, Kebin was permitted to return to the office. His coworkers noticed that he was quieter than before and often worked late. His manager was caught off guard when, standing next to his favored floating foosball table, Kebin had expressed concern about the amount of work he had previously delegated to his unpaid intern. After returning to his cushioned work rocker several minutes later, Kebin was overheard lamenting to no one in particular, "She's worked with me for seven months and I don't even know her name."

Tonight, Kebin sat beside the large window overlooking the city as he skimmed through Cheryl's college applications. Grammar had never been his strong suit, but it was the least he could do for the girl, who he learned was working hostess shifts in the evenings to help support her family. His goal was to help Cheryl's essays look as "normal" as possible, which he saw as her ticket to getting into a good school ("They're not going to give scholarships to weird kids"). As it turned out, Cheryl's essays were not only "normal," but deft and literate. Kebin was intimidated. He opened a separate tab in his browser to look up the word "ontology."

He was relieved to finally delete one "foremost" from the two he found existing side by side in the eighth paragraph, happy to have noticed an imperfection that Cheryl had overlooked, to have helped her in some way.

Kebin raised his head as he heard the beep of the sliding doors being opened with a touch ID. It was rather late for any of his coworkers to linger and the janitor always entered with keys.

A strange woman walked through the sliding doors. She was sweaty and disheveled, wearing a camisole, running shorts and flip flops. There was a touch ID in her hand, but Kebin had never seen her before. He decided the woman looked weird but also familiar.

"Louise?" he asked. Louise didn't hear him or pretended not to, making her way over to the long lucite work table beside the office kitchen. A street-art inspired mural towered above her. Kebin walked slowly toward his former coworker. He watched as she unpacked a laptop and charger from her bag. She connected the device, which chimed and lit up as it powered on. Her triumphant fists shot into the air.

Kebin stood beside the work table, waiting for her to notice him. Louise's eyes were fixed to the screen, her fingers rapidly working at the keyboard. Kebin opened his mouth to speak, then paused, remembering his empathy coach's instruction to pause for fifteen counts before vocalizing a thought. He began counting in his head as he watched Louise's face. By the time he counted to thirteen, he had already decided not to engage with her. It didn't seem like she wanted to talk.

Kebin took a cold-pressed mocktail from the fridge and returned to his work station. Shivering, he reached for his sweatshirt. He took one last glance back at Louise, then returned to Cheryl's essay. The sound of his typing joined Louise's, and the muted traffic horns below.

Nine (Alternate)

There was a knock at the front door. Louise felt the warm light on her face. She shielded her eyes as she lifted herself from the floor. Her back cracked as she stretched. Her limbs were stiff as she wiped the drool from her chin, the sweat from her torso. The tarp had imprinted itself on her back, but she would not notice this until later when it was brought to her attention in the light. The apartment was completely dark, the paper taped to the window serving as an effective shade from the stars in the sky, the moon in waning gibbous. She turned toward her front door and winced. Strong light was still coming in through the hole where the knob had fallen off and underneath the door. She walked toward the door, wondering if it was the sound of the knocking or the light that had woken her up. She tugged at the elastic waistband of her underwear, unsticking the fabric from her skin. She checked her watch and the screen brightened. It was 10:10 p.m. She had missed her cop drama serial. The knock came again.

"Who is it?" she asked groggily. There was no response.

"Hello?" she asked again.

“I’m sorry I’m late,” said the voice on the other side of the door. The voice seemed to contain a multitude of voices within itself, like an orchestra. She swore she could hear a flute somewhere, buried in the mixture. The light through the missing knob flickered subtly as they spoke, “I came for the repair, ma'am.”

“Oh, right!” said Louise. She gathered a loose piece of tarp around herself and pulled the door open. Louise shielded her eyes as the room flooded with cool light, as bright as the sun. It was coming from a giant wrench that the repairperson was holding like a staff. The repairperson wore dark goggles, presumably to protect their eyes from the blinding light of the wrench. Louise wondered how they had made it past her landlord, let alone down the street.

“Now,” said the repairperson, raising the wrench and thus dimming the blinding, cool light. She sniffed the air and turned to Louise. “What’s broken?”

The Bather

Car horns blast all day and night, penetrating the walls of a small Midtown bathroom. A sink and toilet occupy the immediate space to the left and right of the doorway. A clawfoot tub is tightly packed behind them on the far side wall. Smooth tiles climb from floor to ceiling. The bathroom walls are particularly thin; the noise from the street passes through them like cotton screens. They rattle as an airplane flies overhead. A skylight centered above the bathtub frames the plane's passage. An exhaust trail lingers in its wake, bisecting the window with a soft white line.

A bather is seated in the tub. She does not see the plane through the window or the exhaust trail as it fades into the sky. Unable to fully recline in the tub, she sits with her bent legs jutting out of the top of the water. She crosses her forearms over her knees and rests her head against them. From this vantage point, she watches the sweat from her face drip down onto her stomach. Her round belly protrudes like a bald island above the surface of the water. In a singularly perfect moment, a droplet of her sweat falls into the pocket of her belly button.

In the street below, several car horns slam in unison. A man starts to scream.

"*Listen*, man! You're not *listening*, man!"

The bather leans back against the tile and recalls a dream. Her eyes close. She is on a sandy beach. Her body lies parallel to the water, a silhouette against vast, mirroring planes of sea and sky. Looking down the length of her nude torso, she notes the resemblance of her breasts to two cracked eggs sitting in a pan. She is ambivalent to the idea of her nipples changing color like yolks in the heat of the sun. A draft at her side indicates that the tide is growing longer. Soon, she will feel the water on her skin. The bather notices sand in the cuticle of her left big toe and reaches down to remove it. Her arm extends gracefully and brushes the sand away. She takes a moment to examine the arm's sculptured musculature before it returns back beside her. She smiles in quiet adoration of the lightness and flexibility of her limbs.

Desiring a deep stretch, the bather pushes her weight into her hands so that her torso and pelvis lift off of the ground. The water barrels across the sand, passing coolly under the bridge of her body. Only her palms and the soles of her feet remain on the ground. She shivers as the water makes contact with her fingers and toes. She relaxes her neck and lets her head fall back towards her shoulder blades so that she is looking down at her arms, her wrists submerged in water. The tide fizzes as it lingers, then retreats back towards the sea, leaving behind tiny bits of foam between her fingers. She smiles.

A distant rustling to her right commands the bather's attention. The noise is distinct from the sound of the waves. Something is moving through the dunes. She hears the rhythm of bare feet treading softly across the sand. The footsteps grow closer. Locked in her backbend, she cannot bring her body back down to the ground. She looks past her hands to the upside-down stretch of empty beach through her arms. The noise comes to a halt. She looks back at the sand beneath her torso. A shadow has eclipsed her own. A stranger's hand rests gingerly on her knee. Her spine lifts, welcoming the touch. The fingertips pulse as they rest on her skin.

As the hand slides along her thigh, her spine arcs further toward the sky. Her heartbeat increases as she feels the warmth of breath between her legs, the sound of a wet parting. Her mouth falls open at the first stroke of the stranger's tongue. A seagull flies down and grazes on her breasts, mistaking them for food. The bather is unmoved, concerned only with the sensation of the warm hands that gently spread her ass apart, and the tongue that runs between her legs, in slow, focused movements, like a dog to a wound. The stranger's lips tug gently, stroking and coaxing her further open. A moan escapes from her throat, sending the seagull flapping back toward the ocean. The bather can picture her body as though from a distance—a piece of architecture, a complete and perfect arch.

"*Listen, man*! You're not listening, man!"

Salty sweat stings her eyes. The shouting pounds the sides of her skull. A car door slams loudly.

"Are you *listening* to me, man?" The man's voice is lost in the blast of a passing truck.

The bather tries to return to the caresses of the stranger. Her bush tickles her hand like soft seaweed tendrils as it lies helplessly between her legs. Her eyes gravitate toward the sink. She thinks of the stroke of the stranger's tongue between her warm legs as the cold tide washes over her toes.

The sink is low enough so that she could hoist her leg out of the tub and bring her foot to rest in the basin. With careful maneuvering of her toes, she could turn on the sink faucet and the cool water would run down the sole of her foot. With one of her legs in the sink, she could better position herself beneath the bathtub faucet. If she turned the faucet on, the water would strike her right between the legs. She can picture it vividly, her pink flesh flapping back and forth under the force of the stream.

Despite her efforts to lift the leg, it refuses to move. She looks at the leg, still pinned in the corner of the bath. She becomes aware of her flesh, confined so tightly by the sides of the tub and the tiled walls surrounding it. She grasps the sides of the bath to use the strength of her upper body to lift herself out. Her body grinds painfully against the porcelain. Her movements are futile, cramming her legs further into the corners of the tub. A small movement occurs below her chest, but it is merely a roll of flesh that has untucked itself only to be replaced by the formation of another.

She sighs and stares resentfully at the trapped body before her. She stares until her vision blurs. Her body becomes a soft pink shape, unbroken by ridges, shadows, dimples or rolls. Another drop of sweat drips from her brow and forces her to blink.

Just as it had when the plane passed overhead, the bather feels the wall at her back begin to rumble. The source, she observes, seems to be within the wall itself. The ceiling gurgles and she looks up. A water pocket hangs like a distended stomach above her. The pocket begins to grow, moving with the unpredictability and appearance of an animal trapped under a blanket. It makes its way across the ceiling and down the wall, pushing the tiles forward as it descends closer toward her.

The tiles imprint little squares into her back as the wall bears upon her. No longer able to sit upright, she caves under the weight. Her head throbs in time with the blasts of noise from the street.

"I *told* you, man!"

She looks longingly toward the sink. If only her leg was free, she could certainly reach it.

The wall continues to bear upon The bather, shoving her toes further into the corners of the tub.

She looks down at her body, stuffed into the tiny bathtub. In the dream she had been so mobile.

The wall presses forward, mashing her breasts into the tops of her thighs. It is hard for her to breathe. She feels her chest expand with each shallow sip of air. She wants nothing more than to shrink, but she keeps growing. The bather wonders if she could collect enough breath so that she could use the strength of her exhale to push the wall behind her back into place. Then, perhaps, she could use momentum to send her body upwards and out of the tub.

The bather flies back with the force of her exhale, shoving the wall back into place. Her leg rips free from the tub, sending a jet of water high into the air and onto the bathroom floor. Cool droplets land on her face.

The freed leg explores the territory outside the tub, eagerly tasting the tiled floor, then the knobs on the cabinet beneath the sink. Rung by rung, the foot climbs and hoists itself over the lip of the basin. Over the bridge of her nose, she watches the toes wander across the sink's silver fixtures. A cold trickle of water starts out from the tap.

As the cool stream licks the inside of the bather's foot, she returns to the beach. The water is above her wrists.

She inflates, feeling her body rise like the dough upon which an entire mold of the bathroom is destined to be imprinted.

"Yep, that's definitely a leak."

The bather's eyes flutter open, her gaze immediately fixed on the ceiling. A man's hairy torso hangs in the skylight, stretching from one end of the window to the other. His paunch jiggles as he speaks. A carpenter to repair the roof, four weeks late.

The lower half of her body begins to quake. The stream from the sink has become torturously cold. The wall behind the bather lurches forward again, shoving her body forward and forcing her foot further under the stream. Her foot attempts to scramble up the side of the basin, but slides helplessly back under the faucet. The bather growls at the face that has been formed by the pair of moles above the carpenter's belly button.

"Listen, man! You're not *listening* to me!" comes the voice from the street again.

She could kill them all.

"Listen man—"

The bather roars and pushes all of her weight against the wall behind her. She is surprised by the strong, echoing crunch and slams her body against it with greater force. *Thunk, thunk, thunk*.

The wall whimpers and slides back into place, but the bather isn't finished. She slams her weight back again and again. The wall splinters away and tiles fall into the tub. Each slam of the bather's body sends more debris tumbling down into the water and onto the bathroom floor. She slams through drywall, concrete, brick, steel, and doesn't stop until there is nothing but a gaping hole left at her back.

The wind caresses the bather's shoulder blades. The hair rises on the back of her neck as her skin connects with the spring air. She tilts her head back into the hole behind her and looks up toward the sky. Cloudless and blue.

The bather sneezes then laughs as she imagines the layer of dust and grime that must be coating her face. She looks over just in time to see the last pieces of her bathroom wall fall onto the pavement below, startling a group of pigeons.

"*Man—*"

The bather grinds her teeth and punches through the remaining wall at her side. It crumbles away, exposing the entire view of the intersection below. Listen Man stands at the center. He is unmistakable, shouting and wildly gesticulating. A car lies angled off of the pavement, leaning into the street in front of him. A gangly teen sits in the driver's seat, visibly unharmed but perhaps shaken. A crushed bakery box lies on the ground between them.

A trail of smeared icing extends from the box to the front wheel of the car, a massacred cake beneath it.

The bather slips her foot out of the sink and down to the floor. She hoists herself up and stands in the tub. The water has become tepid.

She clears her throat. "*You* listen! *You* listen, Man!" Her voice starts barely above a whisper, slowly getting louder with each repetition. "Hey man, I'm talking to *you* man!" She feels her jowls rippling. She screams: "LISTEN, MAN!"

Listen Man shakes his head in dismay at the distracted teen and lets his hands fall at his sides. He turns to look in the direction of the young man's gaze. An apartment complex towers above them. Something is moving along the side of the building. A man in a tool belt scrambles down the fire escape. At the top left corner of the building, a large chunk of the exterior is missing, exposing a view of a small bathroom. The sun moves from behind a cloud and casts more light into the room. Listen Man squints. A woman stands naked in a clawfoot tub. A ring of purple and blue bruises stretch across her hips and her thighs. Listen Man cannot be sure, as he is too far away to read her lips, but it appears she is staring him straight in the eyes.

The Extended Scream

The Extended Scream took place on Thursday afternoon, inside of a Volvo parked on the third floor of a mostly empty parking garage. It was reported to have lasted approximately 31 minutes and 43 seconds. These figures should be treated as rough approximations, however, as the only person who witnessed the Extended Scream (henceforth referred to simply as 'The Scream') was the person releasing it.

The Screamer sat in the driver's seat of the parked car in a semi-fetal posture with his knees drawn into his chest. The posture stretched his anus, causing the latter to resemble a second, howling mouth, silenced by the layers of his clothing as it smushed into the seat. His shoes, removed, remained below.

A small, grimy animal stood at the entrance of the parking garage stairwell. Perhaps once recognizable as a purebred dog, the animal's current appearance could be likened to the bygone elegance of an outgrown pedicure. It watched The Screamer's car in apparent fixation, its vision obscured by the matted tufts of white hair. A small, pink tongue dangled out of a gap in its bottom row of rotting teeth as tiny puffs of its hot breath filled the frozen air. These breaths and the occasional, muffled jingle of the collar around the animal's neck were the only sounds that could be heard outside of The Screamer's vehicle throughout the duration of The Scream. Buried somewhere beneath a tuft of fur, a tarnished bronze tag dangled from the animal's collar. The tag read, in script, "*Tangles.*"

Roughly six blocks away from the location of The Scream, a third and fourth breath were mixing behind the large window of a small studio apartment. A pair of lovers were entwined on a mattress in the corner of the room, their breath invisible in the centrally-heated atmosphere. A globelike lamp on the surface of the desk beside the lovers shook precariously as one of the lovers moved on top of the other. The eyes of the lover lying beneath her remained open, fixed on the ceiling above as though he were witnessing a funeral taking place there. A later examination of the ceiling would reveal nothing but a minor water stain too abstract to resemble anything of the natural world.

The woman stopped and slid off of her lover. She watched him rise slowly from the bed and walk over to the window. The faint blue evening light looked cold as it fell across his face. He stared at the street below for a long time, before slowly making his way back to the bed. A muffled squeak sounded beneath his foot, and he reached down to grab the tiny, crab-shaped toy that was lying there. He sighed sadly and let it fall between his fingers. He looked across the room. She was nearly dressed, adjusting her scarf and hair before pulling the hood of her jacket up around her face. On her way out, she turned back to glance at him. He looked back at her, but it was apparent that he was seeing something else. It was as though part of him still lingered beside the window.

A single tree stood in the street below, facing the window where the man had just stood. Its gnarled branches reached toward the sky, as though demanding the answers to some question. On the front of the tree were the tattered remnants of a poster. Most of the text was gone, but the remaining words conveyed a tone of desperation. A remaining fragment, still stapled to the bark, rippled in a sudden gust of wind. The black and white image featured the side of a well-groomed animal's face—- a tiny eye peeking out from a mass of white fur.

Tangles flinched as the wind blew his hair into his watery eyes. He continued to watch the car.

The man in the driver's seat let out a final cry and collapsed into the steering wheel.

Tangles suddenly remembered a smell that he had wanted to investigate and started back down the stairs. His frail body maneuvered slowly over the concrete steps. When he reached the second level of the garage, his ears perked up. He bolted toward the center of the lot, stopping at a croissant-sized piece of shit that was lying there, perfectly intact. His nostrils fluttered excitedly as he whiffed. Startled by the force of a sudden sneeze, he jerked his body away from the object of his fixation. He shook his grimy mane and coughed as he skittered away along the concrete surface of the lot toward an unknown destination.

Several weeks prior Tangles had suffered a minor neurological trauma that caused part of his face to become frozen into a permanent, smile-like expression. A woman called the number listed on a lost dog ad later that evening to report that she had seen the animal on the other side of town. She hoped that it was of some consolation to report that it had looked as though he were very happy.

No Spoon

Her pen moved behind the clipboard. She switched the crossing of her legs and looked up from her notes. Her gaze bore into me from over the rims of her clear frames. Her pen continued to scratch against the paper. "You know that I don't like when you wear those," she said.

My reflective sunglasses sagged on the bridge of my nose, but I dared not adjust them lest I address my therapist's remark. I straightened myself in the chair, my hands tightly gripping the arm rests. It was a posture similar to the one I'd assumed when Eoghan had brought me on a roller coaster for the first time, nearly a decade ago.

"You know what I'm talking about, right?" she asked. Her eyes flitted back and forth across my reflective sunglasses, searching for my eyes underneath. "We came to the conclusion last time that you don't speak as honestly when you are wearing those."

I remained silent. She frowned.

"If you aren't going to speak, then there is no point in paying for my services." Her pen stopped and she set the clipboard down on her thigh. The water trickled through a pipe overhead. I could hear it rushing toward the heater, where it would emerge as steam.

With a single finger, I pulled the sunglasses further down my nose.

"That's better," she said, picking the clipboard back up and continuing to write. "Now, when did it start?"

"When did what start?"

She sighed. "Last week, we finally started to talk about your habit of stealing and consuming very *specific* types of food."

I shifted in the chair.

"You informed me that you compulsively stole the receptionist's nori-wrapped almonds off of her desk when she went to retrieve the new patient forms for you to fill out."

"She knew it was me?"

My therapist ignored the question and continued, "We looked at pictures of food and you identified which foods you would steal."

"Yeah, I remember."

"You said you would steal all of the foods in each picture, with the exception of the grapes."

"They were seedless," I said. "I could tell that they weren't organic."

"Right. You mentioned this last visit." My therapist brushed a strand of hair out of her face. "Last visit you also mentioned that it hadn't always been like this, that there was a point in time in which you would have eaten all of the food in the pictures, but wouldn't have stolen any of it."

"S'pose I did say that, yeah."

"So, when did it start?"

I fell silent.

Her eyes narrowed and her writing slowed, threateningly.

"It started at University, I guess." I tried to push the sunglasses back up the bridge of my nose and she hissed. I dropped my hand immediately. Her writing resumed its normal pace.

“Look,” she said. “We are nearly out of time today, but there is something that I would like you to try. Consider it homework.”

I sat up in the chair. My interest was piqued.

“When was the last time you went to a restaurant?” she asked.

I thought of Lucy’s smile flickering in the candlelight at the opposite end of the table at the Meditterean place. “Ages ago ... ”

“Ok, here is your assignment: I would like you to go and have dinner at a restaurant. I would like you to keep a journal recording your thoughts as you wait for the food, as the food arrives, and immediately after eating, then again an hour after eating. Can you do that?”

“That sounds easy enough.”

“Good,” she said. “You will, without question have to pay for your meal. Please do not think of doing otherwise.”

The door to the lobby was just on the other side of the room. I could dash right over to it, run straight past the lobby full of waiting patients and their pinging phone games. I could run between the elevator doors and travel down, down, down, and away forever. Then I thought of her hiss. “Ok,” I sighed.

I was too anxious and indecisive about choosing a restaurant, so I let my therapist choose one for me. Immediately upon walking through the solid wood door of the place, I regretted my decision.

“Table for one?” a humorless hostess called out to me from the end of a drafty corridor. Her pointed boots clacked ahead of me as I followed her through the shadowy tavern to a table. Flickering lanterns swung above. I removed my sunglasses to avoid knocking into anything. I was already dubious of the name of the place, *The Hoagie of the Baskervilles*. My therapist had likely chosen it on purpose, knowing I wouldn't enjoy anything on the menu. The woman was clearly a sadist, not only for this reason, but for suggesting I try eating in a restaurant on a Friday night. The place was packed with couples eagerly seeking experiential dates. They stood posing with the mechanical mastiff outside of the restroom and sat nestled into booths with an entire bottle of wine, nothing but a plate of potato wedges between the two of them. No desserts, just the check. They'd linger awhile, laugh at something on their screens, then leave. It was easy to confuse envy for hatred.

"Menu," said a dirty paperboy as he produced a folded menu from his sack and set it down on my table. He held out his palm in expectation of a tip.

"It's just the menu," I snarled and shooed him away. The pocket-sized notebook my therapist had gifted me dug into the leg of my trousers, reminding me of why I was there in the first place. I took it out and set it on the table beside the menu. I searched the menu paper for something to eat and found it:

Peas and Potatoes
Beetroot and Y. Pudding
Parsnip Sampler

The waiter arrived in the midst of my examination of the menu. I ordered the parsnip sampler, the peas and potatoes.

After the meal, the waiter appeared, suitcase in hand. "Desserts?" he asked. Before I could answer, he opened the tarnished latches. I cried out as the light fell on the case's glistening contents. Without my prompting, he began to recite which desserts in the case were additive free. He paused with a gloved finger under his chin as though he, too, were in disbelief.

"I suppose that's all of them," the waiter said. His gaze flitted between the desserts, searching for some miscalculation.

"Are you absolutely sure?" I said, sitting up in my chair. "Everything in the case?" I began to sweat.

"Let me check with the kitchen," he said nervously. He returned and confirmed with a solemn nod that yes, everything on the dessert menu tonight was free of additives, gluten, soy and dairy free. I told him I would take it all. I waved away the dessert spoon in his outstretched hand.

"No spoon for me tonight, my dear waiter."

I watched my server's tweed-covered back hurtle toward the kitchen with the obsolete utensil. I waited until he was out of sight to lower myself into the open case.

The couple across from me was laughing, waving to the paperboy as the waiter cleared their plates. The minute he was gone, they leaned over the table to kiss passionately in the shadows. With an unsteady hand, I raised the razor-blade shaped treacle to my throat.

It hadn't always been like this. I, too, once had someone to dine with, someone to kiss in the shadows. At University, I was active in several student organizations and went to parties. I was well liked and was even involved in a long-term polyamorous relationship with three other students Lucy, Phil, and Eoghan. We were together for two years and four months before they cast me out of our shared apartment. I should have seen the breakup coming, but due to the memory loss provoked by the medication I was pilfering from a Craigslist couch surfer, the last several months of the relationship had been nothing but a smear on my braised brain. Our fridge and pantry were constantly stocked. Produce on the bottom, milk substitutes on the lowest shelf. The others were divided into subsections, organized by a common ingredient or process: hemp, fermentation, dehydration, sprouting, carob, soy, and so on. At first, I was the black sheep of the household. Tomatoes, beans, and toast were what I'd grown up eating and all I'd ever known. A tiny corner of the fridge was reserved for my "American" singles and inexhaustible mayonnaise. One afternoon, I was in the apartment alone with Eoghan. The both of us were seated at the kitchen table, cramming for the 'Shamanism in the post-Digital Era' exam. Eoghan announced suddenly that he was hungry, got up from the table, and went to the pantry. He slid the flour-free crackercreams tray out of its plastic sleeve.

"Oh, those crackercreams belong to Phil," I told him politely.

"Don't worry," said Eoghan. "I'll replace them before Phil comes home. I just need a little something sweet." Before long, Eoghan and I demolished the entire tray. We finished making our flashcards and went through all of the review material, floating on the high of the antioxidants and enzymes.

"We've eaten the entire tray," I whispered, horrified.

"It's good for us," Eoghan said, "Vitamins." He looked at the clock. Phil would be home in the next half hour. Eoghan fled from the table and rushed to the market. He was back, seated on the coach and reading by the time Phil returned home. He assured me not to worry about it later when I offered to split the expense for the crackercreams. From that moment forward, the fridge and pantry had opened themselves to me. I began shopping at the biomarkt and began tasting my roommates' food when they were out. My mayonnaise and cheese disappeared to the back of the fridge. The sweetness of the GMO-free food was only enhanced by the rush and the risk of getting caught. I became bolder. I refined my craft at fluffing leftovers and smoothing the surfaces of no-gurts and natural fruit sorbets to make them appear untouched. As the end of term approached and my studies became more rigorous, I forgot my caution and became sloppy.

I'll never forget the fateful night Phil caught me eating Lucy's hard boiled kelp cakes with my bare hands. Amid a mouthful of food, I desperately tried to explain myself to him. The excuses became completely unintelligible as I began to weep. I knew the consequences of my actions. It had been weeks since I'd replenished the flax noodles and despite my insistence that we adopt a Bataillan model for our grocery sharing policy, my request had fallen deaf on the ears of my closet capitalist partners.

The issue was not so much the stealing, Phil explained as I wept; it was the total lack of respect suggested by the frequency of the incidents. Lucy, who had been eavesdropping around the corner, entered the room and announced that the previous week I had taken three spoonfuls of her lactose-free ice cream without her permission. I knew she was telling the truth because I remembered accidentally coughing up a particle of an also-stolen soy-dog into the container in the process. I saw my grave being prepared in the darks of her eyes as she retold the story. Lucy found my lack of discipline grotesque and thought I'd really let myself go. She could tell I was no longer engaged in our sex life. The other night, she said, she caught a glimpse of us entwined in the reflection of her vanity mirror, and she couldn't help but feel that it didn't resemble "what making love should really look like."

Horrified by the cruelty of her words, Lucy collapsed onto the kitchen floor. Eoghan emerged and took her into his arms. Speaking mostly to Eoghan now, Lucy repeated over and over again that she didn't truly mean what she'd said, she was just angry that, once again, I'd taken her food without her permission and rendered it completely inedible in the process.

"It's a shame," Eoghan said. "You used to be so creative—always thinking about poems, but these days we only see you parked flat on your arse in front of the fridge or on your way to a biomarkt or to *Nan's Tired Again* to get your fix."

I stared at Phil, Eoghan, and Lucy. They thought that they had just delivered the speech that I needed to turn my life around. In truth, I couldn't think of anything but Nan's. My hands tingled from just the mention of it.

As we said goodbye, Phil reassured me that his attraction for me would never die. He shuddered as I went to put my hand on his back. I smiled and adjusted my scarf as if to insist, "I'll be just fine," or whatever one might say to provide others with a sense of comfort when one has forgotten how to speak.

I left a tip for the waiter on the table and made my way out of the *Hoagie of the Baskervilles* restaurant. The gesture of leaving a tip made me feel a little less guilty about putting the cash that had been sitting under someone's else's plate into my pocket. After all, I couldn't truly taste any food unless it was stolen.

"Wait!" a voice behind me called out.

I turned slowly, certain that I'd been caught.

It was the waiter. "Your diary," he said breathlessly. I took the notebook from his outstretched hand.

I stepped out into the cold evening air, and although I was no longer hungry, I didn't feel satisfied. There was a familiar fire burning within me. Once again I found myself staring at the neon logo above the entrance to *Nan's Tired Again*. Two personified bogs—Heathcliffe and Topsy, the *Nan's Tired Again* mascots—flashed me their neon faces from inside of the letter "A." Nan's was the only all-organic English-owned grocery store in town.

I felt the serotonin rush immediately upon stepping through the automatic doors. A thief's paradise, there were no sensors or cameras in Nan's, only an elderly woman—Nan herself—policing the exit. Occasionally, she checked the customer's receipts, but usually she just looked in their shopping bags.

"You can't choose a proper apple worth shit," she once said to me after craning her wrinkled neck to peer into my bag.

Tonight, however, it seemed that Nan was not in attendance. My body tingled with excitement as I walked through the aisles. I would pay for a few groceries like an honest person, and stuff what I wanted to steal into my trousers. I grabbed three boxes of raw crackers, American flavored nutri-puffs, herbs, spreads, and clean jams. I was careful each time I unbuckled my belt, looking over my shoulder to make sure no one else was around. I checked my appearance in the reflection of a refrigerator door. My stuffed pants looked just as lumpy as the rest of my body.

Rounding the corner toward the dairy section, I tripped and nearly fell flat on my face. I looked down at the object I had collided with; a large bundle of blankets in a variety of colors and textures lay on the tiled floor in front of me. The bundle rolled over, revealing a face. Two glassy eyes held me in a confrontational stare.

"Pardon me," I apologized. "I didn't realize you were lying here."

The face stared wordlessly back. Though the size of the bundle suggested the body inside of it was that of an adult, the face resembled the unworldly disposition of a newborn child. The bundle erupted into a loud spasm of coughs, spraying my face and shirt with what seemed like an unreasonable amount of phlegm for a single person to produce. When the coughing fit was over, the face resumed its froggy expression. I wiped my face with my jacket sleeve and turned the body back over the way I'd found it. I grabbed a no-gurt from the case beside us and headed toward the checkout counter.

Beate, my store crush, was working at one of the registers. A leather jacket draped across the chair behind her. A collection of deep purple and red lipsticks sat beside her register. I had watched her put on this same jacket and apply one of these same lipsticks many times as she would close for the day. Her excitement to leave the store to get on her motorcycle and go somewhere less tragic was palpable. Once, I had worked up the courage to chat with her, asking what she kept in her fridge at home.

"I don't know," she had said, glancing at me nervously. "Beer. Nothing."

As I waddled towards Beate, the bags of puffs in my crotch produced the soft sound of boots breaking fresh snow. I set my items down on the conveyor belt.

"I'm dead," Beate said without even looking up. "Next register, please." Reluctantly I walked over to Greta's register. Likely, she would bore me with the details of every television show she'd watched this week. Perhaps if I were more attracted to her, I'd care to listen.

"There's a man with a baby's face who's lying on the ground in aisle sixteen," I informed her before she could begin talking. "He's covered in blankets and has been projectile coughing on the customers. I figured I ought to let you know."

Before Greta could respond, a deafening blast echoed from somewhere in the store. A beam of light came down through the ceiling and shone unto aisle sixteen. Greta and I watched in silence as the bundled person began their ascension toward the source of the light. Faint trumpet music began to play and the heavenly sound of a woman humming filled the store. The blanketed person's mouth was plastered into a grin as they rose higher and higher into the light. A splattering cough echoed through the store as the beam of light faded and the bundle vanished.

The store returned to its fluorescent glow, visibly unchanged by the whole affair. Greta looked mournfully at the spot where the bundle had disappeared.

"Auf wiedersehen," she whispered, then proceeded to ring up my order.

"Store's closed. Please take your purchases to the register," yelled the manager as I walked toward the exit. He was speaking to no one, as I was clearly the last customer.

As I passed through the sliding doors, I stole one more glance at Beate. I noticed that she was crying as she counted the money in her till. I waited for her outside of the store in hopes that she would accept my offer of a free-trade tissue. Moments later Beate emerged. Freshly applied makeup ran down her face because she was still crying. She noticed me and walked over.

"I was supposed to go to the staff party tonight after work," she sniffed, "but I think I'm too sad to do much of anything."

"What's the matter?" I asked

"This sounds crazy, " she said, starting to collect herself as she blinked away her tears, "but I think the man that was taken up into the sky just now was the only man that I have ever loved."

"Well," I said, "what's so crazy about that?"

Beate said nothing.

We sat down on a bench.

The remaining Nan's staff emerged from the store.

"Hey, Beate," called the manager. "We're all gonna carpool to buy some *crazydrugs* before the party. We only have room for one more in the car in the car though." He looked at me, then back to Beate. Greta was standing behind the manager; her eyes bulged as she noticed me sitting next to Beate.

"I don't think I really feel like going anymore," Beate said.

"Bummer," says the manager, "Would you at least want *crazy-drugs* for the road?"

"Yeah, why not," she said, her accent emerging, "I'm ravaged by grief." She took the silk pouch from the manager's extended hand. The manager licked his teeth and flashed the "rock on" sign before piling into his smart car with the rest of the staff.

"I have a motorcycle," Beate sniffed, "I can give you a ride home."

"Ok," I said, anxiously eyeing the small bike.

We threw my groceries into the compartment beneath the motorcycle's leather seat and Beate climbed on. The stolen biscuits crunched in my pants as I sat behind her.

I took the drugs but felt nothing at first.

That's my house, I said, pointing to the concrete slab on the other side of the street.

As I climbed off the bike I realized that the bags in my pants had ripped open. An outpour of puffs, crumbs, and bits trickled down my legs as I stood. My head was spinning. There was nothing I could do to stop it. Fine crumbs filled my shoes and spilled onto the ground all around me. I accepted defeat, standing in a pool of naturally flavored dust. Beate stared at my pant legs and the growing pile of orange puffs around me. I had the feeling, watching her eyes, that she, too, was starting to trip.

Real Teacher

His suit was new. His shoes, clean. He boarded the train and chose an unoccupied seat toward the front of the car. After securing his luggage overhead, Daniel sat down. The light inside the train made it difficult to see anything beyond the window, so he stared at his reflection. His gray duplicate looked more tired than he felt inside. There was something about the light on trains that brought a harsh edge out of every softness. He thought of children sleeping beneath the flickering fluorescents of the subway, how the shadows aged their faces. Only in the past two years had he become a frequent subway rider. Before the crash, he had driven everywhere.

The accident haunted him regularly, both in waking life and dreams. He had been on his way to work, a daily commute on the freeway. He wanted to move away from the city to be closer to work, but Stella didn't like that idea. It was the source of frequent disagreements. You hate the job anyway, she'd sigh, why move when you can just quit and find something better? He had washed the Volvo that week and vacuumed the interior of the car the night before. It didn't solve the problem, but having a clean car helped make the commute more bearable. Daniel glanced in the rearview mirror and saw a motorcycle behind him. The motorcyclist was a hulking figure in a leather jacket, their face completely obscured by a reflective black helmet. As the motorcycle cut in front of the car, Daniel noticed that the motorcyclist was not alone. A woman sat behind the cyclist, so closely pressed against them that Daniel hadn't noticed her at first. His eyes widened as he noticed the familiar knot of black hair flapping up and down at the base of her neck. An emerald-green pin reinforced the hairstyle at the elastic, flashing as the traffic slowed slightly.

The woman turned around and saw him. The whites around her eyes grew in sudden recognition. Her lips moved as she said something to the motorcyclist that made them drive faster. Stella turned away from Daniel so violently that her hair came loose, fluttering behind her like spitting, mocking tongues. Her large duffel bag was strangled to the back of the bike with a bungee cord. He couldn't understand. He had seen her just that morning.

The sensation of falling backwards became physical. Without realizing it, Daniel had started to ease his foot on the gas, increasing the distance between himself and the motorcycle. Cars behind him began to honk. Drivers leaned out of their vehicles to flip him off as they passed. Daniel's foot remained still. He sat in the driver's seat, face unchanged as the cars collected in front of him and washed away the traces of the motorcycle and Stella. He glanced into his rearview mirror only in time to see the automobile hurtling towards him. He shuddered as he remembered hearing the loud rubber squeal, the crunch of metal on metal.

Daniel jumped as the whistle blew and the train lurched forward. The train burst forth into the light, an assertion of speed and progress. Trees whipped past in the window beside him like a blur.

"Tickets," sang the conductor, pausing at Daniel's seat. A silver hole punch glinted in their hand. Daniel retrieved his ticket from his front pants pocket. They examined the ticket.

"Thank-you," the conductor sang.

After Daniel had submitted his two weeks notice, his boss had stopped speaking to him. The tired, distracted man hadn't even uttered so much as a congratulations, nor—as it came time for Daniel to leave—a goodbye. As Daniel stood before the glass office door, his boss raised his head and gave a nod of acknowledgment, somewhat bitter. He was used to such interactions by now. Stella had left him behind in a similar absence of closure.

As houses flitted past in the window beside him, he smiled as he thought of the hundreds of mounting miles between himself and the life he was leaving behind: the old job, the old boss, the old apartment (which he'd always liked, though the heaters never seemed to work so well in the winter), and the memory of Stella. Lately, he'd found himself wishing that he could tell her how much things had changed. He wished she could see him now.

He reached into the backpack at his feet, producing a leather-bound folio full of pages of coursework. "The Whole Child," read one article; "Teaching through Silence" read another. A full color brochure slipped out from the stack of black and white pages. Daniel removed it and studied the familiar cover, a hand-drawn image of a sprawling brick schoolhouse, a greenhouse and horses in the background. In the foreground, a group of children stood on the lawn, arms linked together. Above the image, a rustic font read, "A School Among the Trees: The Wheywort Institute."

Arrival

The train began to slow as it approached the station. A green-roofed platform rose into view, clouds blooming above. Daniel searched the crowd for waiting faces. Near his window stood a woman smoking a cigarette. Could this, Daniel wondered, be his driver?

He was off of the train, then beneath the shade of the platform, facing the possible driver. She smelled more clean than the mountain air itself.

"Mr. Daniel?" she asked.

"Just call me Daniel," said Daniel.

"I am the driver from the Wheywort Institute and will take you and your belongings to the faculty housing." She looked at the bag over his shoulder, then the small suitcase in his hand. "Is this all you've brought with you?" she asked.

Daniel nodded.

"A fresh start," he said.

"A fresh start," repeated the Driver as she stamped out her cigarette.

The Driver drove a blue Mercedes with a red leather interior. A little figurine—a seated person with arms wrapped around their knees—jiggled on the dashboard. The figurine's plastic head was clear and full of a heterogenous mixture of blue water and yellow oil. When the road became rocky, the colors would mix to green and the figure would tilt forward as though they were going to be sick.

"Do you know how to drive?" asked the Driver. Her eyes were hard-focused on the road.

"I have a license," Daniel said, "but I don't drive much these days."

"Oh?"

"I was in a car accident two years ago and didn't feel eager to drive afterwards," Daniel explained. "I'll drive again soon, once I settle in."

The Driver nodded empathetically. "Well, if you ever find you need a ride, I am happy to give you one."

"Thank you," said Daniel, "that's very kind."

"You're very lucky to have earned a job at the school," the Driver said. "Very beautiful place, great teachers. If I have children someday I'd want them to go to a school like Wheywort. It's a gifted school, you know. Remind me, where were you teaching before?"

"Nowhere yet," said Daniel, "Wheywort will be my first formal teaching job."

"What did you do before?"

"I was a consultant for a chemical company," Daniel said quietly.

"You didn't like it?"

Daniel wondered if the Driver would try to talk to him throughout the entire duration of the drive. Perhaps she was an anxious driver and needed to talk. Yet she looked so confident behind the wheel; she maneuvered the winding country road as though she'd designed it.

"I wanted to do something more meaningful than sitting at a desk all day. I'm not sure that I can, but I'm going to try as hard as possible to teach the students something valuable. Even math can be a vehicle for teaching so much more. People don't often consider science and math as things that can help foster critical thinking skills, but I think, if you frame things properly and integrate thoughtful material into the curriculum, you can communicate more than one valuable lesson. If all else fails, I hope to at least impart them with the gift of solvable equations. In a world in which there are no absolutes and relationships are fleeting, there will always be math to turn to."

The Driver nodded.

"As a chemical company consultant, I was only hurting others," Daniel continued, "I couldn't sleep at night. A coworker's son drank thirty ounces of one of our products on a 'take your child to work' day. He died, right there in the lab. I applied to teaching programs the next night."

The interior of the car darkened as the trees became more dense, enclosing the vehicle in a green-roofed tunnel. Then, as suddenly as it had happened, the landscape opened up and the rolling hills and blue sky burst into view.

The Driver gasped suddenly and the car swerved. A butterfly with iridescent blue wings had flown into the car and was now perched atop the steering wheel. Its wings fanned slowly up and down between the Driver's pale hands. Daniel leaned forward to remove the apparent source of the Driver's distress from the steering wheel.

"NO," thundered the Driver. Daniel recoiled, startled.

"I was only going to set it free, release it through the window," he explained.

"Let me slow down first!" commanded the Driver. She pulled the car over to the side of the road and stared at the insect on the steering wheel. With a nearly invisible movement of her wrist, the Driver hit a switch and the car windows rolled down with a mechanical hum. A fragrant breeze replaced the leather scent of the car's interior. The butterfly, indifferent to the human distress around it, continued to sit on the steering wheel.

Daniel wanted to reach for the butterfly, but was afraid of upsetting the Driver. He opened the door of the car and stood up to stretch his legs. Queen Anne's Lace was growing at the side of the road, just past his feet. He had the sudden urge to pick a piece for the driver but decided against it. He leaned to look into the car. The driver's eyes were still fixed to the steering wheel, her white knuckles still gripping the parking brake.

"Here," he said as he reached toward the steering wheel. He gently coaxed the butterfly into his cupped hands. He offered the butterfly to the pasture in the distance and it immediately flew out of his hands. When he got back in the car, the Driver was smiling at him.

Faculty Housing

It was dark when a sign marked Wheywort Institute appeared in front of the Mercedes. Silhouettes of buildings flickered faintly through the trees, illuminated by the occasional porch light. The darkness pleased Daniel, as such were the ideal conditions for stargazing.

A small building emerged on the left side of the road.

"Here," the Driver said and turned the car into a large, gravel parking lot. She turned off the car and the soft Motown she'd been playing on the road disappeared. The faculty housing was just up the hill, too steep for cars to drive up. Despite Daniel's protests, the Driver threw his heavy bags over her delicate shoulders with surprising strength. He began to sweat through his clothing as he followed up the path in her effortless wake. At the top of the hill were a few small houses, similar in size, Pre-Civil War era in style. Daniel immediately favored the last house on the left. It seemed to have a charming rust-colored facade, but it was difficult to tell in the dark.

"That's your house," the Driver said, pointing to it. They ambled up the front porch to the door, which the Driver used a large key to open. She dropped the bags inside with a thud. She flipped on the lights so the wood paneled, rustically furnished room came into view.

"Where do you live?" Daniel asked the Driver.

"In town," she said. "I like the distance."

They stood together for a moment in the darkness. The Driver seemed to be waiting for something. It was hard to identify the mysterious expression on her half-illuminated face.

"Goodnight, Daniel," she finally said.

"Goodnight," he replied, but she was already halfway down the hill.

A School Among the Trees

The Wheywort School was alive with the scents and signs of school back in session. A fine trail of pebbles and dirt crunched beneath Daniel's feet as he followed the principal to his future classroom. A large bag of soil with its top ripped open sagged at the far end of the hallway. The principal quickly acknowledged Daniel's interest in the bag.

"We try to combine textbook knowledge with real-life skills wherever possible," she said, directly quoting the mission statement from the school's website. "That's why the children are learning horticulture in French."

Daniel nodded as he listened. He noticed a row of drawings that had been tacked up on the walls. The principal, again noticing his interest, paused to let him take a closer look at them.

"Rice paper," she said proudly. "The children make the paper with the Geography teacher. Our students can't progress into elementary school until they have demonstrated basic natural paper making skills and are strong enough to lift a basket full of one hundred and sixty eggs on their own."

Daniel opened his mouth, but the principal continued.

"You'd be surprised how many students have a greater struggle with the latter than the former."

As the principal turned, Daniel noticed a pink pipe cleaner and a single red carnation had been woven through her hair. The arrangement was quite haphazard; the carnation stem had been broken in several places, suggesting that the flower had been inserted into the principal's pinned hair with some difficulty. The pipe cleaner also seemed out of place with the rest of her attire, a flattering khaki-colored pantsuit. It suddenly occurred to Daniel that a child had likely done the principal's hair. He chuckled at the thought and imagined the principal patiently waiting as the clumsy bodies and tiny hands maneuvered around her. If the principal happened to smile, she was careful not to let anyone—-especially the children—notice.

"Magnificent," she'd say as she turned her head side to side, examining herself in the small mirror the children presented to her.

Daniel turned to examine the rice paper drawings more closely. Each composition had a similar format: a few handwritten sentences in clumsy late Gothic script at the top, followed by a small illustration at the bottom. An example on Daniel's right called to him. The composition seemed more sophisticated than the others. Figures labeled Mom, Dad, Moo and Emma (Babysitter) were cowering beneath what appeared to be a kitchen table. Above them, a car was pulling in through an open door. The door and the car were slightly smaller than the figures, indicating that these objects were positioned further back in space than the rest. Atop the car stood a small boy. His scowl was represented by a small dash below his nose. In the boy's right hand he held a gun, which he was using to shoot large, round pellets into the air. Vicious-looking dogs or perhaps wild pigs (it was difficult to tell) flanked the car. The boy's eyes were orange scribbles. Daniel re-read the caption above the image:

Me when I don't get what I want.
By Combo, Age 7

He squinted at the text. A comma in red ink had been inserted after the word me, presumably by the child's teacher.

At that moment, a very small child appeared in an open classroom doorway. It stared at Daniel and the principal with large, bug-like eyes. The child managed to move forward in spite of its feet, which were turned slightly inwards as it waddled towards them. The child stopped at Daniel's knee.

"Beads!" the principal exclaimed. "How lovely to see you. How are you this morning?"

"My sister's tooth is about to fall out," said Beads. "She can wiggle it back and forth but she's not allowed to try to pull out at school. She lets me touch it sometimes. It is very loose."

"How interesting," the principal said. "Beads, may I ask what brings you here?"

The child stared at Daniel.

"This is Mister Daniel," the principal said. "He is going to be observing Mr. Grey's class."

"That's my sister's class," said Beads.

"That's right," said the principal. "Beads, if you do not have a purpose for being in the hallway, where should you be?"

The child avoided her gaze.

"Beads?"

"In my classroom."

"Goodbye, Beads," said the principal sweetly.

"Goodbye, Beads," said Daniel.

"Beads is one of our most gifted students," said the principal after the child disappeared. "His sister, Cobb-Ann, not so much, but she is a very sweet girl."

"I'm sure she's lovely," said Daniel.

The principal was not listening. "Shall we?" she asked. "I'll take you to the classroom now.

She knocked softly on the door at the end of the hallway.

"Yes?" yelped an anxious adult voice on the other side. "Ah—the door is open!"

The door swung open before the principal could open it. A young man about Daniel's age stood at the back of the classroom. His suit matched his prematurely graying hair. Thirteen students ranging between the ages of six and seven sat grouped into tables of threes and fours. It appeared that they were working on a graphing assignment. Dice sat on the tables. All eyes stared at Daniel.

"Xtopher," the young man in the suit called, "thank you for opening the door for the principal and her guest. You may have a seat now." Xtopher emerged from the other side of the door and returned to an empty seat beside a young girl that looked remarkably like Beads, but larger, stronger. She was perhaps the largest student in the class, sitting almost a head above her peers. This, Daniel thought, must be Cobb-Ann.

"Hello, children," said the principal. "I'd like to introduce you to Mr. Daniel. He will be helping out in the classroom starting tomorrow."

"We *kno-ow*," sighed a bespectacled child at one of the further tables. The principal did not acknowledge the impoliteness of the student's interjection, but her face changed momentarily as though she had smelled a foul odor. Another hand went up in the air. The principal brightened.

"Yes, Jingle?"

"Um ..." Jingle shifted in his seat, suddenly shy in the spotlight. "Is Mr. Daniel a real teacher?"

"After Mr. Daniel's six month observation and assisting period, he will be eligible to become a head classroom teacher," said the principal. "Mr. Daniel is a real teacher, however, in the sense that you must treat him with respect. You must follow his orders, just as you would Mr. Grey."

"Exactly," agreed Mr. Grey, who was suddenly standing at the door, beside Daniel and the principal. He was peeling a tangerine over the compost bin with noticeable difficulty. The skin came off in tiny shreds and fell outside the basket.

"Lydia wasn't a real teacher," said Xtopher.

"Yes she was," snapped Mr. Grey, without turning to look at the child. "If you would like to make a comment, please raise your hand first."

"Who is Lydia?" asked Daniel.

"Mr. Grey's former teaching assistant," said the principal.

"It's a pleasure to meet you Daniel," said Mr.Grey. He swallowed the peeled piece of fruit whole.

There was something pitiable about Mr. Grey. As Daniel looked into the teacher's eyes, he had the sensation that he was standing at the door of a haunted house. He looked older, more tired up close.

"It's a pleasure to meet you as well," Daniel said. Then, turning to address the children, "It's a pleasure to meet all of you."

The principal smiled and said to the room, "Mr. Daniel and I will be going now to fill out some paperwork and finish our school tour. He will see you tomorrow." Mr. Grey's eyes flitted nervously to the departing party.

"Does Mister Daniel have a moment to meet during our recess? A brief chat?" There was a hint of desperation in his voice. The principal pulled a leather-bound planner out from the inner pocket of her suit.

"We'll be visiting the astronomy lab around that time," the principal whispered sadly. "Perhaps the two of you can arrange to meet at the end of the school day? If Mr. Daniel is willing to stick around for an extra hour?"

"Certainly, absolutely," Daniel said. "I'll stop by."

Mr. Grey smiled gratefully, the happiness transforming his face into something less tired, more youthful.

"What do you think?" the principal asked Daniel as the door closed behind them.

"The children seem lovely," said Daniel.

Daniel staggered up the hill to the faculty housing, happily exhausted. Under his arm was a hefty folder of documents, which he was supposed to complete and sign by his first day tomorrow. His legs ached, but the sensation was satisfying. The other faculty houses were apparently occupied, but Daniel had yet to see another teacher emerge from one of them. bicycle was chained to one of the porches. As quickly as the thought had crossed his mind, a man appeared in a front door, lighting a cigarette. His friendly wave to Daniel was tinged with an air of suspicion. Daniel returned the wave, happily.

The man walked to the edge of his front porch, smoking as he watched Daniel. Getting the sense that the man intended to speak with him, he walked over.

"Good afternoon," said Daniel as he approached the porch.

"Good afternoon," the man said, his dark eyes still appraising him.

"Daniel," Daniel said, stretching out his hand.

"Martin," said the man, returning the shake.

"I'm the new assistant in Mr. Grey's classroom," Daniel explained. "It's my first day tomorrow."

"Mr. Grey's classroom," Martin repeated.

"Yes ..." Daniel said. He eyed Martin curiously. With his large stature and with cool, mildly intimidating demeanor, Daniel supposed he was a security guard.

Martin smiled, as though reading his mind. "I'm the After-School Coordinator," he said, letting out another exhale of smoke.

"Is that so?" asked Daniel.

The men stood in silence on the porch for a moment. The sounds from the forest filtered in.

"Mr. Grey's class is not an easy class," Martin said finally.

"Really?" asked Daniel. "The children seemed fine, quite sweet."

"I don't really know many of those kids, but I've definitely heard about them." Martin said. "Most of Mr. Grey's children have been banned from taking after-school classes."

"What?"

"Like I said, they don't tell me much." Martin stamped out his cigarette in an ashtray on the window ledge. The men looked out at the schoolhouse in the distance. The parking lot was beginning to fill with cars, parents coming to collect their children. "Looks like I'm running a little late today," Martin said. "It was a pleasure to meet you, Daniel." He shook his hand. "I'm just a few doors down if you ever need anything."

The steps creaked as Daniel made his way up his porch, but he didn't hear them. He was thinking about his conversation with Martin. He found it unusual that the children were banned from after-school activities, especially because punishment and exclusion were vocally discouraged in the school curriculum. If true, what had warranted the decision to ban an entire classroom? He had forgotten to ask Martin if he ever needed a hand. If there were a tennis team or something of the sort, he would love to coach it. It would be a shame if his own students couldn't join. Perhaps he could convince the principal to let Mr. Grey's class back into the program.

The afternoon sun stretched across Daniel's living room. He looked forward to the opportunity to come home from work and read in the dappled golden light. The old building was in remarkably good condition, though the presence of the occasional late summer grasshopper might reveal an insulation issue. It was something he'd look into before the weather grew colder. The antique furniture was not his style, but he found it charming. His favorite was the rocking chair with its mustard-yellow cushioned seat. He sat down in the seat, releasing a full-body yawn. Soon his eyelids were heavy, his body was sinking. Strange thoughts and visions floated through his mind, acquiring mass, becoming dreams.

He was in his old car, the Volvo, driving on an empty road. The scene filled him with a familiar sense of dread. A motorcycle materialized in front of him, the same one that he had seen on the day of the crash. Stella was seated on the back. Her arms wrapped around the driver. Her hair whipped free. She turned around to look at Daniel. She was laughing.

The motorcyclist turned their head. Their eyes were orange scribbles. Stella's mouth shrank into a cartoonish "O" as they pushed her off the motorcycle. Instead of tumbling down, her body floated off the road and landed softly in green pasture. Daniel's Volvo sped onward, still tracking the motorcyclist, whose body was still turned around to face him. The cyclist lifted their helmet and red locks of hair spilled out. The motorcycle driver was the Driver.

"Hi," the Driver called out.

"It's you!" Daniel cried joyfully.

A giant cloud blotted out the sun and the road grew darker. The Driver and the motorcycle were gone. Daniel became nervous. He heard a small hacking cough behind him and turned around. A child sat in the backseat.

"Please cover your mouth," Daniel begged the coughing child. "I work at a school now. I can't afford to get sick." The child glared and coughed harder, producing a visible cloud of mist. Daniel turned forward, but it was too late. The road was gone. The vehicle tumbled off the side of the road. Stones and branches pummeled the sides of the car as it fell. The car finally landed with a solid knock.

Daniel woke with a start. It took him a moment to realize that he was not in a darkened ditch, but his living room. The knock came again. Daniel rose cautiously from the chair and made his way to the door. His body felt stiffer than before. To his surprise, it was the Driver. She looked very clean, as though she had been polished. Her hair was neatly twisted into a hairstyle that exposed parts of her neck that Daniel hadn't seen before when it was down. She wore a silk brown dress, and apparently, nothing underneath it. The exposed skin on her chest and arms looked as smooth as the fabric.

"Hi," said Daniel.

"I was wondering if you'd like to get a drink in town with me tonight," she said.

"Tonight?" asked Daniel.

"I can give you a ride home... if you'd like."

He looked over her shoulder and saw that her car was parked at the foot of the hill. The engine was still running and the headlights were on. A muffled melancholy tune drifted up to the porch from the car radio. A metaphor for his libido, he thought bitterly. His immediate inclination, however, was to decline the invitation. He wasn't a big drinker, but this had nothing to do with it, as he enjoyed having a cocktail from time to time. Something else was holding him back. The image of Stella on the back of the motorcycle floated through his mind. She was laughing louder and louder.

The Driver shifted in her dirty white sneakers. He had to give her an answer.

"I'm sorry," Daniel said, "but I can't tonight."

The Driver looked more disappointed than he had anticipated.

Ok," she said sadly.

As he watched the Driver trudge across the lawn back toward her car, he was overcome by the uneasy sensation that he had forgotten something important. The car door shut and the sound of music became louder: a mournful, dated tune with a timeless sentiment. The ornament on the Driver's dashboard jiggled green as she pulled out of the driveway. *I'll be waaaaiting*, the song wailed, *fooooor you to come byyyy*. The singer's voice distorted as the car curved around the bend and into the distance.

It hit him. Daniel had completely forgotten to visit Mr. Grey after school. He thought of the unusual yet tragic teacher, the sheds of citrus peel gathering on the floor, the desperation in his eyes as he asked Daniel if he had time to meet at the end of the day. Daniel checked his phone. No missed calls. He wandered to the laptop in the other room. No emails either. It was dark outside. Perhaps the matter wasn't so urgent after all. Daniel typed out a quick apology to the teacher, stating that he would be available by phone throughout the evening. At this point, it was the best he could offer. He returned to the chair and sat down, reassured by the weight of the phone in his pocket.

A call woke Daniel in the early hours of the morning. The sky was still dark, but the birds were chirping. He rolled over in bed to switch on the light.

The principal was on the other line. She sounded tired.

"Daniel, I am so sorry to wake you," she said. "There's been an unforeseen event and you will have to fill in for Mr. Grey tomorrow, possibly indefinitely."

"Oh?" said Daniel.

"Yes," said the principal. She fell silent for long enough that Daniel thought connection had been lost. There was a strange crackling on the other end. "He was a wonderful teacher. Even the note that was found next to the pills included instructions on how to proceed with today's lesson plan."

"Oh, dear," said Daniel.

"The show must go on," she sighed sadly.

Daniel remained silent.

"We have complete confidence in you," said the principal. "However, we will be sending in an experienced substitute to help you with managing the classroom. It can be a lot for a single teacher to handle on their own." The receiver crackled again and Daniel realized she was crying.

Daniel hurriedly washed himself and walked to school in the darkness. School didn't start until eight, but he wanted to be there well ahead of time to prepare for the day. A security guard named G let him in.

"I've got the faxed copy of Mr. Grey's instructions right here," G said, handing Daniel a stapled packet, "I didn't read the instructions or anything, but everything in the classroom should already be labeled for your convenience. Sure is a shame that Mr. Grey decided to pack up in the night." She waited for Daniel's response, but he remained silent. "I'm sure he'll be much happier in Wisconsin," she continued. "I guess when you really need to go, you have to go. "

Daniel hurried up the stairs. The hallway felt eerie in the pale morning light without students or teachers. It smelled of bleach and flowers. An elderly janitor waved from the end of the hall. Daniel waved back.

He entered the classroom. The chairs seemed so much smaller without the students in them. He sat down at Mr. Grey's desk and turned on the fringed lamp beside it. Immediately, the room felt closer to the inviting space he recognized from the day before. He wheeled back in the chair. Little post-it notes had been pasted on the desk drawers, clearly marking "lesson plans," "first aid," and "homework." There was a folded note on top of the desk. In identical script, it read, "Daniel."

Around eight o'clock the first parent arrived to drop off their child. Daniel set his third cup of coffee down on the reading rug with a slightly trembling hand and rose to greet her.

A mother in a pale pink coat stood in the doorway with a brooding child. Daniel immediately recognized the child from the roster as Sage.

The mother looked curiously at Daniel.

"Is Mr. Grey out today?"

"Yes," said Daniel, "I'm the new assistant teacher, Mr. Daniel. I'll be filling in for Mr. Grey today." He was unsure if he should mention the possible permanence of this situation. It seemed as though the parents had not yet been notified.

The mother brightened instantly. "Ah, Mr. Daniel, it is a pleasure to meet you. Sage told us about you the other day."

Daniel looked down at the child, whose arms were still angrily folded over his chest.

The mother sighed. "We apologize, but we are having a difficult morning so far. We really didn't want to wear clothes today. It is unsanitary and inappropriate to be naked at school, but we seem to forget and then we throw a big fit before we come to school."

The child stamped.

The mother, speaking more to the floor than to Daniel, continued, "Yes, we are seven—"

The child stamped harder.

"Yes, we are *six years* and *eleven months* old now and *still*, this is a daily struggle for us." The mother's gaze lingered on a stain on the carpet as her son instinctively went to his worktable. Sage squinted at the morning message Daniel had written on the chalkboard, then went to retrieve his folder.

"We'll work on it together," Daniel said, turning back to the mother. To his relief, the mother smiled. With his words, Daniel had instilled her with confidence in him as a teacher, an image of which he wasn't yet fully convinced of himself.

Daniel walked around the desks as the children worked at their assignment. Within minutes there was fidgeting, pencils were dropped. A student by the name of Hamila let out an exasperated sigh and let her head fall onto the desk.

"Hamila's not doing her work," Jingle immediately reported.

Daniel waved away the concern and encouraged the student to focus on his own assignment.

"We are choosing a character from our reading books that has a character flaw, then using evidence (he pointed to the word, which was written on the board) or examples from the story to explain why we think so," he reminded them. "We have one more minute to write down at least one character flaw and then we will be moving onto the second part of the question."

The chatter continued. There was giggling from the far end of the classroom.

"Cobb-Ann!" Daniel called. "Please stop wiggling your tooth!"

"How do you know my name?" asked Cobb-Ann through her fingers, visibly surprised.

"I know all of your names," said Daniel. The children stopped and fell silent. It seemed that he had finally unlocked the key to gaining back power in the classroom.

"I memorized them," Daniel continued. "That's how I'm able to fill out this attendance sheet." He held out the blue paper for the children to see. It was clear from their silence the children had not noticed him fill it out.

Cobb-Ann stopped wiggling her tooth and put her hands under the table. For the next few minutes, the children quietly worked on the writing prompt. A quiet student, Rosy, raised her hand. Her name had been marked with an asterix on the roster. The note from Mr. Grey beside it read, "Reliable."

"I need help," Rosy whispered as Daniel knelt beside her desk. They read the prompt together. She couldn't understand the concept of a character flaw. It was too abstract for her to understand. Daniel racked his brain for an example.

"A flaw doesn't mean a character is bad. In fact, most people have them," he explained. "Flaws make a character more human, but may cause difficulty for the character or those around them. Flaws aren't something a character has on purpose. In fact, they might not be aware that they have a flaw. That's often where the conflict of a story happens. Does that make sense?"

The child stared at Daniel.

"I haven't read this book, but I'm sure if we—"

"You haven't read our community reading book?" cried Hamila.

Daniel turned to face the child, who was halfway across the room. "Well, no—I—"

"He's not a real teacher, he's just an assistant," said Tathiba, shaking her head in disapproval. The volume of the children's voices rose. Some shouted. Xtopher began to lean dangerously back in his seat again. Another student, Grabe, unzipped and zipped the fly of his pants, repeatedly flashing his penis to his classmates. Daniel hurried over to tell the child to stop, but was immediately distracted by Rosy's arm as it shot straight up into the air. Her fingers were fully extended, indicating the urgency of her announcement. Daniel called on her.

"Look at Cobb-Ann," said Rosy in her gravel voice. Daniel wheeled around to find Cobb-Ann covered in blood, proudly cupping three teeth in the palm of her outstretched hand. She laughed at Daniel as he looked at her, a jet of blood squirting from the new gap in her grin. It seeped down her chin. Where was the aid the principal had promised him? Cobb-Ann maneuvered her tongue to squirt the blood at her classmates. Her hyperactive tablemate, Roger, stood out of his seat, trying to catch it in his mouth.

Daniel, on the verge of fainting, suddenly recalled a note Mr. Grey had written next to the class roster:

Henry: allergic to bees and dairy. Cobb-Ann: hemophiliac.

"Cobb-Ann, please excuse yourself to see the nurse," said Daniel. "Take the hallway pass."

"There is no nurse," she replied

"Yes, there is," replied the other students in unison.

"Cobb-Ann, please go to the office. You need medical attention." He noticed Rosy gazing nervously toward the other side of the room. She waved her hand for Daniel's attention and pointed at Xtopher, who stood at Mr. Grey's desk. Daniel's work bag, which he had left closed on the chair, was now open.

Daniel called, "Xtopher! May I help you?"

The child pretended not to hear him and looked at the floor, smirking.

"Xtopher, please put my phone back in the backpack, where you found it. This is absolutely unacceptable."

"I don't have your phone," Xtopher protested. His left pocket sagged with the weight of the object.

"Xtopher, I saw you take the phone. I can see that it is in your pocket right now."

"I don't have it," said Xtopher. His tablemates giggled

Daniel left Rosy's table and made his way to the desk where the child was standing. His foot hit something hard and he fell to the floor. The lights went off.

"Please turn the lights back on," Daniel called as he attempted to lift himself onto his forearms. He felt a sudden weight on the back of his calves, then another at his lower back. His arms gave way beneath him. Behind him, someone giggled.

"Remember this weight, Danny," another voice whispered.

"Nobody calls me Danny," Daniel snapped. He was startled by anger in his own voice.

The lights flickered back on. The weight lifted from his legs. Daniel quickly got up and brushed himself off.

A loud knock sounded from the other side of the classroom door. The visitor did not wait for an answer and pushed the door open. A tall gray-haired woman stood in the doorway.

"MS. ANGELIQUE," the children cooed. Their demeanors changed completely, more similar to the children Daniel remembered from the day before.

"I'm Angelique, the fourth and fifth grade teacher," said the woman, ignoring the children. "We've been hearing quite a bit of commotion from next door. Is everything alright?"

Daniel felt a sharp stabbing pain at the back of his leg and winced. "Yes, everything is fine! Ah—we've had a student who has lost a tooth—several teeth. Can we have someone help escort her to the nurse?'

Cobb-Ann offered her palm of bloody teeth to Ms. Angelique.

"Good Lord, Cobb-Ann!"

Ms. Angelique called a fifth grader out of the class to escort Cobb-Ann to the nurse. She craned her neck out of the door to watch as they walked down the hallway. "Don't touch her, Cobb-Ann! Don't touch her!" she called after them. Ms. Angelique turned back and scanned Daniel's classroom with her eyes. The children were sitting neatly. Ms. Angelique smiled, apparently satisfied with what she saw. "Is there an aide with you today?" she asked Daniel suddenly.

"No, not yet. The principal told me that Gretchen was supposed to join us this morning."

Angelique frowned. "Gretchen sometimes is late," she said. "I'm next door by myself today, but don't hesitate to reach out if you need anything. I can only imagine how tough today must be on Mr. Grey's kids. They must be so sad to find out that he picked up and left for Idaho just like that." As if on cue the children began to whimper.

"There, there," said Ms. Angelique. "Now children, I want you to be on your best behavior for..."

"Mr. Daniel."

"Yes, for Mr. Daniel. He's your teacher now. Whatever he says, goes."

The children continued to whimper, "Please stay with us, Ms. Angelique."

Ms. Angelique lingered in the doorway. Her brow furrowed as she glanced around the room. "Are you sure everything is alright?"

Daniel felt the pain again at his calf and turned around. Xtopher was hiding under the table behind him, a pencil in his outstretched hand. He locked eyes with Daniel and mimed stabbing himself in the throat with the writing utensil.

"Absolutely," Daniel said to Ms. Angelique. He forced himself to grin.

The teacher smiled, satisfied. "Good luck," she said to Daniel. As soon as the door clicked shut behind her, the children sprang from their seats. Again, Daniel was knocked to the floor. He rolled over in time to watch a circle of small bodies gather around him. Something soft brushed against his arm. It was Sage, stark naked.

"Stop this instant! Sage, put on your clothes! Are you trying to get me arrested?" Daniel cried.

Roger took his character assessment worksheet off of his work table and mashed it into a ball between his hands. The children tightened their grip on Daniel to keep him still. He resisted, but they forced his mouth open. He gagged as Roger shoved the assignment inside. Daniel stared at the ceiling fan above him, hearing the sounds of more paper being crinkled. Rosy cried out from across the classroom. The ceiling fan disappeared from view as shadows closed in on him.

The Aide Arrives

The door swung open again, this time revealing a young woman.

"I'm sorry I'm late," she mumbled. She didn't introduce herself, but there was no need.

"Gretchen!" the children cried out. The tiny pairs of hands that pinned Daniel to the floor relinquished their grip and raced to their seats. Daniel quickly helped himself onto his knees. He paused to loudly hack the wet paper out of his throat. The room fell quiet as he gagged and coughed.

"Gretchen! You're here!" he said, using the edge of the students' work table as leverage to help himself up. As he finally stood at full height, he caught a glimpse of himself in the mirror beside the doorway. It took a moment for him to recognize himself. Little shapes and letters had been drawn on his face in magic marker. His hair stood on end, his widow's peak pulled up by the many popsicle sticks that had been hot glued into his hair. He made no attempt to move them. "Gretchen, I've gotta tell you, we are just so happy that you're here!"

Gretchen looked fresh out of her undergraduate studies and extremely hungover. A button in the middle of her blouse had been skipped and the milky, iced beverage in her left hand was half finished. In her right hand, she clutched a white paper takeout bag. The smell of the warm food drifted through the classroom. The children eyed it curiously, hungrily.

Daniel inhaled and exhaled deeply, loudly. The children began to shift away from him, suddenly afraid. "That smells dee-licous!" cried Daniel. He grabbed his work bag off of the chair and started to laugh. He stepped slowly backwards towards the block shelves and the large window above them. "You'll be happy to know, Gretchen, that we're already ahead of schedule for today! We've finished our writing assignments in record time, finished our poetry books, our Latin exercises, and now we are just about to get out our supplies for geography! I've got a lesson plan for today right there on Mr. Grey's desk. Uh-oh! It looks like the lesson plan is on the floor. Someone must have ripped it on accident, but that's okay—nothing a little scotch tape can't fix, right Xtopher?"

Xtopher stared at Daniel. "We didn't get to our Latin exercises."

"And what a lesson plan!" Daniel interrupted. "What a thorough plan! Notes from the chief himself! Mr. Grey—such a thorough and helpful guy. It's such a shame that he just moved to what are we saying now... *Indiana? Ah, yes, that he moved to Indiana so suddenly!*" Daniel lifted himself up onto the top of the bookshelf. The open window was at his back. He took a sidelong glance over his shoulder. A large tree branch curved in towards the building, just below the window. "You know what's wild Gretchen, is that I came to school very early today to read Mr. Grey's notes and I found instructions addressed to me for the rest of the *year*! It seems like Mr. Grey has been planning on 'suddenly' going to Indiana for a *long* time."

Gretchen was sweating as much as the iced drink in her hand.

"Hey, before we get started with geography, would you mind doing me a favor and keeping an eye on the class? I need to excuse myself to use the restroom."

Before Gretchen could respond, Daniel slipped out of the window and helped himself onto the branch below. The old tree was knotted and perfect for climbing, though his loafers weren't ideal. He heard Gretchen above, struggling to regain control of the classroom's attention.

"Let's play a transitional round of Simon Says," he heard her call. The children cheered. A transitional game, Daniel thought. Milton was elected as Simon, a bad choice.

"Simon says, do whatever you want!" he heard the child call as he continued down the tree. There was a roar of small voices and the window pane above him rattled. The commotion went on and on.

"You have to tell them to stop, Milton!" he heard Gretchen cry.

"Stop," said Milton. The rattling continued. Laughter. The child was clever.

"Milton!"

"Ok, Simon says stop!" cried Milton. The rattling ceased.

"Simon says," Milton paused, "do whatever you want, *forever*!"

Daniel flinched as the children screamed. The screams traveled, possibly indicating that some had left the classroom. He was about halfway down the tree now, but one obstacle remained. He would have to pass by the library window on his way to the ground. He paused above the slightly open window and listened for activity inside. He heard nothing and continued down. As he passed the window, he noticed with dread that a class was in the library, stationed at the very far end of the room.

A teacher was reading a picture book to the students. Their backs were turned to the window. They seemed like good children, completely enraptured by the picture book. A girl who had trouble concealing her excitement rocked back and forth on her knees. The teacher said something to the child and she sat back down. There seemed to be no frustration or resentment from either party.

Suddenly a child broke free of the group and headed toward the box of tissues sitting on the window ledge. Daniel's heart thundered into the tree.

The child, oblivious to Daniel's presence, approached the tissue box and took one with a dramatic, swirling movement of its arm.

Thank god, thought Daniel.

At that moment, the child shifted its gaze to the window. Its large eyes locked on Daniel.

"Beads!" Daniel whispered.

The child seemed neither surprised nor alarmed to see him.

Daniel made a pleading gesture with his hands, then pressed a finger to his lips.

Without removing his gaze from Daniel, Beads lowered his head to catch the wet collar of his T-shirt in his mouth. He began to chew on the garment.

Was this a vow of silence? Daniel continued down the tree. He landed on the grass below with a soft thud.

A mountainous view unfolded before him like a 19th century landscape painting. He would run from the school until he was as faint and blue as the mountains in the distance. He came across the faculty parking lot and was astonished to find a car with its door left wide open, keys still in the ignition. It was Gretchen's car. The licence plate said so: GRTCHN.

No matter how he pictured it, he couldn't get himself past the idea that his escape fantasy began with stealing the young woman's car. Perhaps it was the first car she'd ever owned. Perhaps it was the first big purchase she had ever made for herself. He shuddered. It was a Volvo. Daniel imagined driving the car off road and into the uneven terrain of the forest; rocks and branches clattering against the sides of the vehicle until it became as smooth and polished as a stone washed ashore, all traces of its former resemblance wiped away.

Stairwell

I can't remember the last time I stood at the bottom of the stairwell and it was this quiet. My downstairs neighbor is probably lying in her bed, listening and waiting for me to make noise on the stairs. More than once, she accused me of stomping over her head in "party shoes" at odd hours of the night. It's a strange claim since I can't remember the last time I wore anything but slippers in the house. It's not my sister—who works night shifts at the hospital and lives next door with her four year old son—who is making the noise either. My sister thinks it is because of our downstairs neighbor that the door to the roof is always chained shut. She will find a new place to live with her son and her girlfriend when the lease is up. She says she has saved up enough for a first and last month's deposit.

Communication between my head and feet does not go well. We thump, squeak, and creak up the stairs. Moving more slowly does not reduce the noise. I would love to tell my downstairs neighbor to go to hell, but unlike my sister, I can't afford to move. I did not realize how late it was. If R. hadn't been so late, I wouldn't have had so many drinks. I thought that since we were having so many drinks, that we would go home together. If I had known that we weren't going to go home together, I wouldn't have had that third drink at all. R. took my number and said they would really like to see me again. Unfortunately for R. I have other prospects. Three at least, maybe more since I left the restaurant. If R. texts to say goodnight, I will wait a long time to respond and it will be to say something like "sorry, just saw this" but really I think it is best to not say anything at all.

After they betray me on the stairs, I cannot trust my hands and feet to work together. I will have to sit down to take off my shoes. I walk past my slippers, past the shoe rack in the hall, and onto the door mat. My keys turn in the lock without opposition, which is odd because I can remember locking the door before I left. Maybe, in a rush, I had forgotten. If only I had realized there was no reason to hurry. Nobody shows up to dates on time unless they are desperate. R. arrived over forty minutes late.

I find it strange that anyone would want to meet up with an attractive stranger they met online, take them out for multiple drinks, and not try to hook up with them afterwards. Maybe that was R.'s plan, but I said or did something that made them change their mind. I can't think of what else it could be. My hairstyle has changed from my pictures, but my body is more or less the same. In one photo, I am squatting beside my nephew at the park in a way that shows off my legs. I blurred out his face for privacy, but my sister told me not to use it because people might think that I have a child. I didn't have another picture that showed my full body, so I drew over it with an arrow that says this is not my child.

I have not heard or felt my phone buzz, which probably means that I have not received a goodnight text from R. They did say that they wanted to see me again, so it wouldn't be out of place for them to do so. R. seems like the type that would follow up, but I can't make assumptions; I never would have thought that someone who made a living as a life coach would leave a date waiting over forty minutes on account of the "traffic." R. claimed that when I left for the bathroom, the waitress had given them a look that said you really blew it this time. I thought that R. was just joking, then our separate checks came and it turned out the waitress never charged me for the glass of wine I'd had while waiting for R. to arrive.

R. doesn't post any photos of their body. Perhaps they are religious.

I close the door behind me and sit down on the bed. There is a light shining on the far side wall. It is a reflection from the vanity table in the other room. It is strange because I can remember turning the lights off before leaving. I take my boots off and instead of putting them on the shoe rack in the hall, I sweep them under the bed with my feet. A shadow flickers over the light on the far side wall, probably the cat running around. I wish I could ask her to turn the light off, but I think that even if she had hands, she still wouldn't do it for me, not even if I asked nicely. My foot brushes something soft. It is the cat, sitting at the end of the bed. She stares in the direction of the source of light. Her ear twitches. I sit up. There is rustling in the other room.

My first instinct is to text R., which is probably a bad idea. My second instinct is to call my mother, which is also probably a bad idea because she will panic if I call her in the middle of the night. It is better to investigate first. I creep toward the other room and peer around the corner. The light at the vanity table is on and someone is seated in the cushioned seat. I see my nephew's face in the mirror. He is applying a thick coat of tangerine lipstick around his mouth. The lipstick once had a smooth edged point, but now the creamy blade is worn-down flat. Though his movements are confident, it is clear that my nephew does not have experience applying lipstick. He had probably seen his mother put lipstick on a friend and say open your mouth, because this is exactly what he is doing. My nephew's mouth is stretched open wide and he is getting as much lipstick on his little square teeth as his lips. He frustratedly wipes the lipstick off of his teeth only to repeat the same mistake just seconds later. It is an expensive lipstick, but it is not my favorite shade.

I do not know why my nephew is here instead of next door with the babysitter. The bedroom door hangs open. I forgot to close it all the way. A sliver of light from the hallway shines in through the crack. Through the open slit I can see the shoe rack and a pair of scuffed pink sneakers—too small to be mine—that have been clumsily dropped between my clogs. At least my nephew was abiding by the no shoes in the apartment rule. I close the door and turn the lock quietly. I return to my position at the corner

My cat watches me and I watch my nephew. My nephew's short hair stands on end and he delicately uses my brush to smooth it, but the brush barely touches his hair so he is mostly stirring the air. He puts his fingers directly into the eyeshadows and rubs blue and green onto his eyelids. Next, he opens the powder box and a giant plume of dust rises from the lid. He sneezes, the poor thing. Our eyes meet in the mirror. He turns around on the cushioned vanity chair and stares. I stare. It goes on like this for quite some time. His eyes move critically toward my iridescent midi dress, down to my pedicured feet. Slowly I venture back into the other room to my bed. I turn on the nightstand lamp and decide to read here until he is finished. The light from the other room goes off and I hear my nephew hesitate at the corner as he checks to see if I am watching him. When he decides that I am preoccupied with my magazine, he comes out and unlocks the front door. As he does this, I steal a quick sideways glance from over the top of the magazine. The sneak is wearing my sequined blouse and organza wrap. I had almost forgotten I had them. The sleeves bell long past his fingers. It takes him such a long time to get the door open that I consider getting up to help him, but then I hear the lock click out of place. He pauses before the open door.

"GoodnightAuntLisa," he says through gritted teeth. Lately, his teeth are always gritted when he speaks. We are not sure why, but are in conversation with a speech therapist about how to correct it.

"Are you sure you have to leave?" I ask. There are a million questions I want to ask my nephew, but this is the only one that comes out. He sways back and forth for a moment before answering.

"Yes," he says through gritted teeth, "MyCarIsWaiting-ForMe." I wonder at what point my nephew decided his makeup was satisfactory. He leaves the door open as he goes into the hall to the shoe rack. He takes my white sandals and velcros them tightly at his toes and ankles. He returns to the door and closes it hard before I can say another word. I hear him trudge down the stairs. The door swings back in his wake. He does not close the door tightly enough. I hear a honk down below in the street and race to the window. A yellow cab is outside, grey exhaust running in loops. My nephew emerges from the apartment with the caution of a baby deer, walking in my sandals. He gets in and the vehicle speeds off into the night. I lock and bolt the door and slide into bed. I feel a buzz at my side and the blanket glows blue. It is R.

> R: Hey (1:03AM)
> R: Goodnit! (1:11AM)

In a way R. wins by sending a text that is difficult to respond to. The "Hey" is inviting, but the "Goodnit!" that follows is finalizing, closing. The entire eight minutes of time that passed between their first and second text sits like a phantom between their messages. If I say goodnight, R. might get the impression that I am interested in seeing them again and if I say anything else, it might come across as a desperate attempt to initiate conversation. In truth, if R. were to ask to come over, I would hop in a cab, but this is not what they are asking. They are not asking, because they do not want to listen. They are saying hello only to say goodbye, a mirror of our interaction this evening. For R. sending a goodnight text might be second nature, like opening the door for the elderly woman on their way into the restaurant or leaving an especially generous tip for the waitress;

indications of the wealthy, trauma-free upbringing they boasted about over drinks. What are manners but little learned gestures motivated by guilt and self-preservation. R. doesn't post pictures of their body because they probably don't feel like they need to. Either way, I couldn't care less as I have no interest in going on another date with R. I can't think of a single text that would change my mind.

Meter-Wide Button

The Longshelbys

Thirteen years ago, Dominique Parks met Fleetwood Mac enthusiast Collin Longshelby in the back corner of an apocalypse-themed birthday party. Dominique arrived wearing an elaborate costume she had painstakingly hand-made the night before, believing that it set her apart from the majority of the guests who came dressed as victims of radiation-poisoning. Most of these costumes were similar in execution, featuring smeared dirt across cheeks, torn clothing, and bandaged limbs. A few more committed individuals had fashioned extra appendages to their bodies. A young man on the opposite side of the room fumbled with a styrofoam mutant head velcroed to his shoulder. He seemed oblivious or willfully ignorant to the fact the velcro wasn't strong enough to hold the head in place. Dominique watched his last hopeless attempt before the head came loose again, dangling from a string off his shirt like a tooth hanging by its last thread. He looked up at her.

Dominique looked the other way. She held her cocktail glass close to her body as she surveyed the room. She held herself and her height elegantly, a head well above the other guests in her heels. She felt glamorous, then remembered her costume. She was dressed as an outbreak of syphilis. Marsha, a former coworker saw her and wheeled over.

"I just don't get the costume, Dominique," said Marsha from her fake wheelchair as she studied the heavily papier-mâché'd creation. "Syphilis has been eradicated by Universal Healthcare. It's no longer a threat to humanity. "

Dominique rolled her eyes upward into her thick eyelashes. "My costume is an antibiotic-resistant strain of syphilis," she said and raised her drink to her mouth. Her papers rustled as she drew an invisible line down the side of her costume with her fingers. "I'm the cause of the apocalypse, not a symptom." She delicately extracted a piece of gum from her mouth and placed it on the inside rim of her unimaginative friend's drinking glass.

The young man, Collin Longshelby, watched the interaction from across the room. Aroused by the intensity of the gesture, he hurried over to introduce himself. Marsha's fake wheelchair nearly collided with the styrofoam head as she flew past him. Originally intending to give Dominique a compliment on the uncanniness of the costume, Collin instead found himself remarking darkly that the party reminded him of how unbearable the actual apocalypse was going to be. The inevitability of the world's destruction was one of his triggers, he admitted, but he was currently working through it with a therapist and found himself capable of enjoying life regardless. Perhaps, he followed quickly, she might care to have dinner at an expensive restaurant?

Despite a five-year age gap and incompatible astrological signs, Dominique and Collin began dating, bonding over their shared interest in the arts and similarly financially comfortable lives. In spite of a mutual ideological opposition to the institution of marriage, they wed and decided to use their combined inheritances to found an artist residency program. The couple agreed that the best place to house the residency would be Longshelby II, a planet that Collin inherited from his parents following his marriage to Dominique. Upon his inheritance of the planet, Collin would immediately change the planet's name to "Sara."

Sara

Though it wouldn't be fitting to describe Sara as hostile per se, the planet's appearance would not suggest that she was planning to accommodate life anytime soon. A thick blanket of pale yellow gas loomed permanently in Sara's atmosphere, lending the planet a somewhat noxious, albeit beautiful, appearance. In a constant state of stagnation comparable to a clogged sink, the swirled layer of gas posed no threat to the planet's land-bound inhabitants. Instead, life thrived below this marble tapestry, basking in the filtered rays of solar nutrients that managed to penetrate through to the planet's surface.

Many of Sara's most scenic views could be found on the Landslide, a giant, fenced-in nature reserve that served as the home to the Longshelby Artists' Residency. Thickets of polar trees grew toward the sky and ice-capped mountains rose high above the horizon.

At night, faintly backlit by distant stars, the sky above the Landslide was a velvety black canvas, emphasized by swirling veins and pools of dark blue and green. From the perspective of an observer standing anywhere on the icy surface, the colorful sky might appear to reflect onto the ground below it. It was the sort of magnificence and beauty that could only be experienced in isolation—a quiet peace that one might have to travel far from home to find.

Resident Artist Tugger Graves felt anything but peace as he stood staring out at the seemingly infinite, barren horizon in front of him. He couldn't be bothered with the nightly phenomena, nor the inch-long piece of thread—a source of recent frustration—that was peeking out from the seam of his intelligence suit. Tugger kept forgetting to clip the wayward thread since its appearance about a week prior. It was the first visible sign of wear in the intelligence suit since it had been gifted to him upon his admittance into the residency almost a year ago.

"MARION!" Tugger screamed. His voice shattered the silence. The echo of his voice split like a multitude of birds flying overhead and into the distance. Tugger was on the verge of crying out again, but stopped himself. In the wake of the last scream, he felt a warm sensation, like liquid spreading, in the back of his throat. Fearing momentarily that it was blood, he shook his mind of the paranoia by assuring himself that he had merely tapped into some emergency reserve of saliva. He choked on the fluid and coughed against the interior of his helmet. The crimson-tinged spittle disappeared almost immediately as it made contact with the self-sanitizing plexiglass.

The Health Monitor embedded in the arm of Tugger's intelligence suit let out a soft beep, indicating that the artist's energy levels had been depleted beyond a recommended continuation of current activity. The tiny faces of a psychiatrist, a psychoanalyst, and a randomly selected Voice of Reason[1] remained paused in expressions of grim concern near the top of the screen. The three faces waited for Tugger to seek their counsel with a swipe of his finger. Annoyed by their apparent concern, Tugger darkened the screen with a short wave of his hand and the trio disappeared from view. "MARION!" He screamed the missing Artist Guard's name a few more times. Suddenly, it occurred to him that his voice might not be very audible from outside of his helmet. Perhaps he was only making himself deaf. His facial muscles melted in defeat as hot tears poured down the sides of his aching cheeks.

Tonight marked the second evening since Marion had left. He was certain, however, that she was out there somewhere, roaming the Landslide fearlessly in the dark. Marion had left her tracking device behind so that she couldn't be found—a move that was ultimately against her Resident Artist Guard Agreement (RAGA). Marion was at home in silence and emptiness. Since she'd become such a warm and frequent presence in Tugger's life over the past few months, he had forgotten the nature of her occupation and the frequent isolation that was part of it. During off seasons, Marion spent long stretches of time completely alone.

---

1. A civilian who is selected at random to provide temporary moral support to another individual. A facet of the Universal Healthcare program, the Voice of Reason Initiative (VORI) is intended to promote empathy and instill a broader emotional vocabulary in its participants.

It was rare, she once told him, that she even met the Resident Artists. She protected them from afar, simply by maintaining the Chain™[2] and occasionally salting the pathways.

Tugger hadn't considered what an exception he had been. He had come to know Marion quite intimately throughout his stay on Sara. He thought about the first time he had ever met her. Shortly after his arrival on the planet, Tugger found himself dealing with a particularly oppressive creative block. In order to clear his head, he went for a walk to get a better sense of his surroundings. He vowed not to return until he had thought of something worthy of exploring in the studio.

A day later, Marion had found him collapsed in a ditch. He was fast asleep and virtually unharmed. Her tracking device had informed her that the Resident Artists's levels had declined suddenly, so she set out to investigate. She would later tell him that upon rousing him, she was surprised by the way he communicated with her. He was relentlessly curious, asking all sorts of questions about her past (many of which she could scarcely remember herself). She was shocked when, just moments later, the artist invited her to share a meal with him in his tiny living quarters. She refused, of course.

Despite Marion's initial resistance and distrust of Tugger, he managed to befriend her. At first the intimacy between them was strictly that of close confidants, but it was only a matter

2. A protective shield that encloses the Landslide, the Chain™ and is invisible to the naked eye apart from the names and photos of the residency's patrons, which scroll across its surface at bi-hourly intervals.

of time before things became sexual. There was a point at which Tugger was concerned that nothing he could make would match the joys he experienced in Marion's strong and passionate embrace. The shared fear that their affair might be discovered was only minor, as they lived in virtual solitude. Their secret was threatened only by occasional check-ins from visiting critics and the routine visits from Dominique Longshelby, the residency's co-founder. As the visits were always announced well in advance, Marion and Tugger had found it quite easy to keep their relations a secret.

Eager to soothe his current distress, Tugger closed his left eye for five seconds—a shortcut he had programmed to activate the intelligent suit's radio. The sounds of *XXX-Factor* filled his ears immediately. DJ Massive X was in the middle of another monologue, his dubbed out voice surfing over a relentless mix of post-apocalyptic Human street-step.

"*Much love to everyone tuning in tonight,*" DJ Massive X echoed over the music. The sound warmed Tugger's ears and neck. "*To be honest, I'd probably have sex with each one of you individually.*" A chorus of literal hounds howled in emphasis the signature *XXX-Factor* sound bite. Tugger waved the radio off, feeling his own inner sad-man melody unmoved by DJ Massive X's good humor.

The light from Tugger's headlamp cast down into the snow, bathing the ice in a soft red light. The Chain™ protected the Landslide, yet Tugger still often felt uneasy at night thinking about what could exist beyond it.

The most recently recorded death of a Resident Artist on Sara was eight years ago, before the Landslide or the Chain™ existed. The remains of a young sculptor had been found floating in a lake, spooking the residency's co-founder Collin Longshelby into approving new artist-protection policies. The policies included the establishment of the Landslide—a sanctuary that housed the Resident Artist's studio and living quarters—and the Chain™. As the Frequently Asked Questions section of the Resident Artist Safety Agreement (RASA) stated, the Landslide was the only area of the planet that the Resident Artist was permitted to explore.

Tugger was informed of the sculptor's death very casually, after he'd already accepted the residency offer from Dominique Longshelby.

"What do you mean, *gruesome* death?" Tugger had asked, failing to conceal his alarm. Dominique sighed. It was clear she hadn't expected her words to affect him this way. He pressed her with his silence.

"They found his body floating face down in the water," Dominique said. "There was a clean slit up and down the back of his suit. Whatever got him must have sliced him open and sucked him out like an oyster."

Tugger must have appeared terrified, because Dominique immediately set down the paperwork.

"It was such a long time ago," she said, "We wouldn't dream of reopening the residency if it didn't seem safe."

"Dominique," he interrupted, "Will I—"

“Please,” Dominique interrupted, “Call me ‘Longshelby’—my married name—it's more androgynous.”

“Sorry, Longshelby...will I be safe?”

“Absolutely,” Longshelby said. “Nothing can harm you in the Landslide, especially with Marion, our Resident Artist Guard, there.” The smile faded from Longshelby’s face as she moved closer toward Tugger and lowered her voice. Her expression had become serious. “We need you here, Tugger,” she said., “Someone has to fill this place with culture with a *capital* ‘C.’”

Tugger glanced out the window and caught a glimpse of Collin, who was busy raking leaves out of his meditation garden.

As he stood on the ice, recalling his first conversation with Longshelby, Tugger imagined how the two of them must have looked to an outside observer. How carefree he must have looked as he signed the paperwork, with Longshelby beaming at him like he was the only other person in the world who existed. Tugger hadn't met Marion yet, but as he scrawled his name at the bottom of the agreement, he had taken comfort in the fact that the Artist Guard would always have his back. After all, it was in her contract.

Marion. He had screamed her name so many times that the landscape seemed to whisper it. He heard it in the crunch of his boots in the snow. Marion marion marion. The memory of his last night with her haunted him as he walked. The lightning in her eyes had suggested anything but his guaranteed protection.

“I didn’t even come,” Tugger had told her. He regretted his words the minute they tumbled hopelessly out of his mouth. He had felt so foolish as he stood in front of Marion in the entryway to his sleep chamber, a thin blanket clutched tightly around his naked body. He could feel the rage radiation from her body. He watched helplessly as Marion threw her tracking device to the stone floor. It fell to the ground with an anticlimactic clatter. Tugger stared in horror at the discarded device, realizing with delay the consequence of what Marion had just done. “You—” Tugger stammered.

“*I*,” Marion hissed, her eyes flashing maniacally, “don't give a flying fuck about the RAGA! You can rot for all I care!”

The morning after Marion left, Tugger’s unharnessed penis smacked cold and limp against his thigh from inside of his intelligence suit as he trudged up to the studio. He stared blankly at his work for several hours before deciding to destroy approximately six months’ worth of drawings. He left the studio and began to walk without a particular destination in mind. He raised an arm toward his face to listen to the tiny counsel weigh in on his current predicament. The brows of Tugger’s advisors were furrowed as they considered his desperate demand: “What should I do now?”

The deepest insight came from the Voice of Reason, this time a young, human woman who looked to be in her mid twenties. She had apologized in advance for being a little stoned, though it was apparent that no one else had noticed.

“You need to understand why Marion is upset before anything else,” she said, interrupting the psychoanalyst mid-speech. The psychoanalyst scoffed in offense. "Longshelby represents everything that Marion is not and has everything Marion doesn't have," the Voice of Reason continued. "Your 'betrayal' of Marion speaks to her deeper insecurities about what she thinks you actually want. Longshelby represents the world you come from, a world Marion cannot logistically share with you."

The psychoanalyst and psychiatrist fell silent and exchanged a look of respect for the Voice of Reason. The Voice settled back as she watched and waited for Tugger's response. A strange noise came from the Voice of Reason and Tugger realized that she had started to eat what looked like plantain chips, a food on the verge of being outlawed due to oil content and packaging.

"Do I have a chance of getting back her trust?" Tugger asked the screen desperately. The Voice of Reason pondered his question amidst the soft sounds of her digestion. A fat tear slimed its way down Tugger's cheek. "Tell me," he begged, "can I win Marion back?"

The Voice of Reason paused and stared sympathetically at Tugger, tracing the rims of his unblinking eyes and worry-creased brow as she searched for the right words. She took a plantain chip back out of her mouth and placed it into the bag, embarrassed by the apparent insensitivity implied by her snacking. Her lips parted as she took a deep breath.

AAAAAAAAAA......AAAAAAAAAAoooooooooooooooGGGGGGGGAHHHHHHHHHH..........AAAAAAAAAAAAAAA.........AAAAAAAAAoooooooooGGGGGGGAAAAAAAHHHHHHH........

Yanked violently out of his reverie, Tugger found himself on the desolate Landslide once more. A deafening siren exploded all around him. Unable to plug his ears, he instinctively clasped his gloved hands to the sides of his helmet. He began to panic. A series of clicks descended down his back as the cooling units worked furiously to combat the sweat pouring down his spine. There was only one thing the siren could mean: the Chain™ had been broken.

Tugger tried to remain level headed. He reminded himself that the moment the Chain™ was broken, anything that entered the Landslide would be recognized by the control panel as an intruder. Annoyingly, as Longshelby had once explained, the intruder alert could be provoked by something as minor as tree branch blowing in from the Wild—anywhere outside of the Chain™:

"In the nearly impossible circumstance that the Chain™ is damaged and something blows in from the Wild, you can silence the alarm by pushing a button located on the control panel," Tugger recalled Longshelby saying as she zoomed in on a map of the Landslide. "The button is easy to find, you really can't miss it."

Disoriented, Tugger ran in the direction of the control panel to silence the alarm. The alarm was so loud that his body resisted his movements. His knees shook, then buckled. Almost there, almost there, he chanted to himself as he staggered onwards. A black object shot past in his peripheral vision, but Tugger couldn't be sure if he had actually seen anything at all. In the oncoming daylight, the ice shone like the surface of water.

The glittering surface reminded him of an afternoon months before, when he had been sitting beside a geothermal pool with Marion.

He held his gloved hands out in front of himself as if to feel the heat of the steam as it rose from the pool.

Marion laughed, then she sighed. "Tugger," she said, "I think I'm happy." Her voice was full of warmth.

Tugger looked into her eyes and his heart surged with joy. He wondered if he should tell Marion that he loved her. His helmet slumped forward awkwardly on his head as the silence settled between them. Would Marion—who had uttered the phrase "happy" perhaps for the first time in her life—understand the significance of a thing so abstract as love? He searched his memory for DJ Massive X's thoughts concerning the term. Everything was love: "Massive Love," "XXXL Love," or "Venti Love."

The only DJ Massive X quote that stood out in Tugger's mind was the one that seemed the most uncharacteristically serious in tone. Tugger recalled hearing DJ Massive X whisper in the midst of a flowing ambient track that had run uninterrupted for so long that the sudden intrusion of his naked, unamplified voice was startling.

"Love is a promise."

Tugger remained silent.

"Can we swim in the water?" Tugger finally asked Marion, breaking the silence.

Marion narrowed her eyes at the pool. "No," she said firmly.

"Would it damage the intelligence suit?" he asked.

"No," she said, "but many of the Resident Artists have defecated in there." She shuddered. There was something endearing, Tugger recalled, about her disgust.

"Why didn't you tell Marion that you loved her?" the therapist asked Tugger.

Tugger thought for a moment. "It didn't seem productive," he said, simply.

"Productive," the therapist repeated in a voice devoid of judgement. "Can you elaborate a little bit more on this word?"

Tugger focused on the memory of what seemed like lifetimes ago as he willed himself not to vomit on account of the torturous siren. Without losing speed, he activated the vacuum straw in his helmet as a preventative measure.

The control panel was right in front of him. He pushed his weight against the door. A small beep sounded as the suction pulled him inside. It was dark and damp in the control panel. Rows of blinking lights and switches lined the walls. Graffiti was scrawled on the floor and ceiling. He scanned the room, heart pounding. Then, he saw it.

The massive, flat-topped button rose dramatically from the console at the far end of the room. Its vast shadow fell onto the neighboring controls, relegating them to obscurity and irrelevance.

Tugger wiped the layer of dust off of the button's surface. Beneath it, someone had crudely written the word *loser* in permanent marker. Tugger stared at the graffiti and pushed the button down with both of his hands. The siren stopped. He slumped to the floor with a cry of relief.

"Conduct assessment of hearing loss," he said hoarsely to the intelligence suit, at which point a series of numbers were repeated back to him from within his helmet. A soft voice calmly informed him that the alarm was so loud that it sanded a nanometer off the surface of his suit. *Minimal damage,* Tugger concluded.

"Intruder detected," announced the garbled voice of the ancient control panel. It occured to Tugger that he was hearing the voice of an engineer, likely long dead. Tugger closed his eyes in a moment of brief meditation before initiating conversation with the intelligence suit, which vibrated with the hum of newly acquired statistics from the control panel.

"Okay, give it to me," Tugger sighed, addressing the control panel. Tugger received no response and realized that he was forgetting to use the specific wording that was essential to communicating with the control panel. "Show me what you're working with, " Tugger clarified. The control panel hummed and let out two loud clunks.

"Intruder data collection *finally* complete," says the self-deprecating control panel, "total pressure change of surface on neutral zone 215.2345 pounds. Estimated weight of intruder—"

Tugger made his own calculation without waiting for the statistics. Whatever had made its way through the shield was heavier than a tree branch, and, even more disconcerting, more than twice Tugger's weight.

"Last recorded location of intruder?" Tugger asked.

The control panel fell silent.

"Conduct location analysis of intruder!" Tugger demanded. The Emergency Detection light turned on in the visual panel inside of his intelligence suit. The light glowed orange: *Danger. Caution advised*. A low groan sounded behind him as the door to the control panel creaked open wider. Tugger's heart sank as he realized he hadn't closed the entrance and shut the valve. A thin shadow fell across the control panel. Someone else had entered the room. Paralyzed by fear, Tugger's mind flashed to an image of Marion standing proudly atop their favorite hill.

"Marion?" Tugger croaked.

Silence.

"I'm afraid not," said a voice entirely unfamiliar.

Tugger turned around.

A creature about seven feet tall stood at the entrance to the control panel. Its head and torso were hunched atop two peggish legs and malformed feet. The creature resembled what it might look like if a human was turned inside out, had its protruding organs shaved off, and then stubbornly sustained an outbreak of the most socially crippling adult acne. Viscous pus oozed like Elmer's glue from various enlarged pores all over the creature's slick, moist skin.

"You speak just like a Human!" Tugger gasped.

"Oh yes," the creature grinned, flashing a set of chipped, carnivorous-looking teeth. The creature's voice had a striking resemblance to a long-deceased British comedian whose name Tugger couldn't remember.

"You're...Human?"

"Not quite," the creature said and waited for Tugger to provide another guess. When he didn't, the creature sighed, lost the accent completely and said, "Let me guess. They didn't tell you about *us.*"

"No," Tugger managed to reply. He remembered when Longshelby thrust the 64-page RASA into his lap and how hurriedly he'd skipped over so many of the sections. *Section V: Planetary History, Flora and Fauna, The Wilderness and Its Inhabitants*, flashed before his eyes as he thumbed through the booklet, searching for *Materials and Supplies, Budget, and Universal Healthcare.* What a fool he had been. The creature took a few stuttered steps forward, clearly relishing in Tugger's apparent discomfort.

"My people have been roaming the surface of this planet for a long time. Before us, only intelligent algae thrived here. They started a radio program called DillBeat that still airs on Wednesday evenings. Often, it's pleasant. *My people* have a far greater history of cultural contributions. We were kicked out of the Earth Alliance Thespian and Comedian–Actor Guild (EATaCAG) for our 'offensive' jokes and banished from Earth to live in exile on this rotten planet. We were forgotten until the Long shelbys bought the planet and employed us under the table. We entertained their family for generations. We did everything from stand-up to uncanny impersonations of inanimate objects." The creature snarled. "Let me tell you, it certainly wasn't easy to come up with new material under such harsh restrictions. There are only so many times you can imitate a tissue box before becoming clinically depressed. As exiles, we don't have the privilege of

Universal Healthcare." The creature paused, grasping the sides of its sticky skull in a gesture of agony. "Can you imagine what it was like to come up with new material everyday while being prohibited from making jokes about women?"

Tugger glanced quickly toward the door behind the creature, the dawn of the new day so inviting yet so far away. Interruption of this history lesson would be his quick and absurd death.

"But so far from Earth, there is no longer any need for reason. I feel no guilt, no shame, no remorse. On the opposite side of the Chain™, I am the shark looking into the bowl teeming with little goldfish. They swim around all day and night with such energy and no real purpose. I do not strike, for it is rarely worth my energy.

"The Longshelbys started to realize the planet was changing us, but they did nothing. They put on their intelligence suits and left us to fester under the Grand Greasy Spot." The creature sensed Tugger's confusion at the reference to the Grand Greasy Spot and clumsily made a motion toward a darker swirl in the sky. "The atmosphere changed us. The foods changed us. We became irreversibly eccentric; our tastes became questionable."

"How?" Tugger interrupted.

"The only thing our changing bodies began to crave was untainted human flesh straight from Earth! It was the only thing that didn't taste like stale Jaffa Cakes to our transformed palates. Do you know how the Longshelbys thanked us after we started to eat a few of their artists?"

"Er—"

"They kicked us out, built a shield around their stupid Artists' Residency programme!"

"Well—"

The creature roared, its voice beginning to sound increasingly inhuman, "We think your art is trite. You have a library of 1,000 books and an entire database at your disposal and you make work about the fucking sky because, let me guess, it reminds you of a painting?"

"Actually—"

"Have you any idea how many people before you have made art inspired by the same damn thing?"

"I—"

"Your art sucks so much that my sister and I flipped a coin thirteen ways to figure out who would be the one to break the shield and remove your hodgepodge installation! I was the winner of the final round! I came here to remove your joke of a project and figured that while I'm here, I might as well eat you."

"You—" Tugger's voice cut out as he barely dodged a lethal swipe toward him, resulting in a visible gash in the left arm of his suit. The hazard light appeared on his visual panel to notify him of his current stress levels. Annoyed by the redundancy of it all, Tugger made a mental note to mention in his negative review of the residency program should he be lucky enough to live beyond this moment.

"What if I just agree to take it away? The whole 'damn' installation?" Tugger asked. The creature furrowed its brow as it considered Tuggers proposal.

"No, that won't do. I can remove it myself! Also, I want to bring your body back as a trophy." He smiled and lunged toward Tugger. Entangled in a furious blur of limbs and teeth and slippy bits, Tugger concentrated on keeping his hands and feet away from the creature's gaping mouth. Threads of thick saliva glinted between its teeth.

Tugger pushed a finger into one of the creature's pus-filled boils, releasing a projectile stream of white ooze high into the air. The liquid came down and splattered onto the front of his helmet. The creature let out a howl of anguish. Tugger found himself suddenly free, on his elbows and knees, crawling like a soldier across the surface of the ice. The snow beyond the control panel was a cruel retardant, but adrenaline pumped him full of unprecedented strength and speed.

Suddenly, he was grasped by the ankle, but the sleek exterior of the suit made him hard to grasp. He gained several more feet before he felt himself being lifted into the air. Tugger looked down at the snow, finding himself helplessly hanging over the shoulder of the horrible creature like a corporate blazer. Tugger thrashed and screamed for a few seconds before the creature became annoyed and slammed his helmeted head against the ice. Everything went black.

***

"So tell me about this installation you're envisioning," Longshelby said as she poured herself a glass of wine during another one of her routine visits to Tugger's studio. The large circular window at the far end of the room framed Longshelby's silhouette and provided a view of the outdoor workshop where Tugger was building a model of the installation he was planning to erect in the center of the Landslide.

"Well, one of the things that struck me the most about being here was the sky," Tugger said, pausing nervously as Longshelby began to leaf through the flat file. She sorted through the drawings quickly, occasionally holding them out in front of her or up to the light with her arm fully extended. Tugger felt exposed. The increasing frequency of the studio visits with Longshelby versus the decreasing frequency of the visits with guest critics was unnerving. When she came to visit in the evenings, Longshelby would bring her own wine. On this occasion however, Tugger had started to drink long before she arrived.

"It's kind of like being underneath a giant painting...the sky, I mean," Tugger struggled to explain, nervously finishing the last of his own glass, "I guess a lot of the work I've been doing is inspired by that. Considering the toxic as ..."

"This is beautiful," Longshelby interrupted as she raised a drawing to the light, then placed it back into the flat file. She shut the drawer, then turned back to Tugger. He could tell she wasn't listening, and with a slight spasm of her ankle as she moved toward him, Tugger realized that she, too, was drunk. Longshelby paused just a few inches from his face. Neither of them wearing an intelligence suit, Tugger was overwhelmed by the sensation of the physical proximity of their bodies. Tugger was convinced he could feel Longshelby's breath on the bridge of his nose and her heartbeat through his pulse, though this would have been impossible. She smelled faintly of cedar and sandalwood.

"Tugger, have you ever choked anyone before?" Longhelby asked. Tugger felt his ears redden as he struggled to answer the question.

"Yes," he said slowly, "but not to death."

"I mean in a sexual context." Longshelby said impatiently as she flicked a pencil shaving off of her dress.

"No, I don't think I would be into that kind of thing," he said. He choked on his own spit., "Is that what you're asking me?"

"I'm asking you to have sex with me, Tugger" she said simply, "and to pull my hair at the very least!"

Tugger glanced at Longshelby's hair: thick, close-cropped curls that framed her face. It seemed enough for at least a small fistful, but the nonspecificity of her request threw him into self-doubt. Perhaps Longshelby preferred a small, concentrated tug to a full-handed grasp. The surface area of her scalp was suddenly vast and terrifying. He glanced out the window, paranoidly scanning the surroundings.

A small glow in the folds of the blanket strewn across the chair beside him caught Tugger's eye. The source of light was Tugger's tracking device, a simple machine with a display screen depicting a map of the Landslide. Tugger zoomed in on the image by whispering the phrase "make my day" into the screen, and in the expanded view of the map, he saw a tiny pink dot—Marion's marker—moving slowly along the periphery of the Landslide. She was in the middle of performing her routine maintenance and damage survey on the Chain™. Based on the current location of the marker, it appeared that Marion was over 2600 meters away from the studio. From this distance, it would take her at least an hour and fifteen minutes to get back to the studio, and she wasn't even halfway finished with her route.

"Tugger?" Longshelby asked, "is everything all right?"

"What about Collin?" Tugger asked, pulling his eyes away from the map and back to Longshelby's face.

"What *about* Collin?," Longshelby repeated. "I'd like to know. Have you ever even seen him once during your residency?"

Tugger could see Longshelby's breasts through her shirt. He glanced at the pink dot on his tracking device once more. The moving dot paused briefly before slowly continuing its path along the Chain™. Tugger smiled to himself as he imagined Marion stopping to examine something on the surface of the snow. Perhaps she had paused to observe the sky, as she often liked to do, with eyes full of a melancholy mysterious to him. He shrugged inwardly, then without moving the rest of his arm, waved his hand to turn off the device. To Tugger's surprise, the dot continued to linger on the screen even after the map had disappeared—a glitch. In those last few seconds before the screen went totally black, Marion's marker appeared to beat with a pulse, as though the dot itself was a living, breathing organism. Tugger witnessed the dot's final breath, watching it glow and grow as though it could fill the screen, the room, and swallow him whole in its warm, pink light.

***

A familiar voice cut through the void. "*Put Mr. Graves down immediately.*"

Tugger's eyes opened. The creature above him had stopped moving. He tried to turn in the direction of the voice and was tossed face down into the snow. The snow enveloped his helmeted head in darkness but he was now wide awake, listening to the muffled sounds of a struggle above him. The comedian's anguished cries filled Tugger with a growing sense of optimism. Feeling something above him release, he pushed himself up out of the snow.

A massive Snow Wiffler the size of a small truck stood in front of him. Long tendrils of hair cascaded down its face and body. Lidless yellow eyes gazed out sharply from its protruding wooly muzzle as it stood proudly against the backdrop of the toxic, marbled sky.

"Marion!" Tugger whispered.

Marion stared back into Tugger's eyes as he followed the line of a stray tendril down to her giant paw, which was stamped into the face of the ex-comedian beneath her. With a snort and an adjustment of her claws, the predator's neck was crushed with a sickening crunch. Vivid pools of marbled yellow and green begin to pour out of the creature's ears, hot and steaming as they spread across the surface of the snow. Tugger shivered with unexpected pleasure at the sight of his enemy's elimination.

"Don't look at me like that, Tugger," she said coldly. "I'm saving you because it's my job." She shook the hair out of her eyes. "I think my skin started to dissolve because I disobeyed the RASA by leaving my tracking device behind." She tossed back her mane so Tugger could see the charred skin underneath, then stepped toward him. Her massive form blotted out the bright sky above.

"Marion, please forgive me," Tugger begged. "I'm in hell!"

Marion's dismissive snort rattled the sides of his intelligence suit.

"I have heard this kind of expression before. It is a complaint, a distinctly Human expression. They do not exist in my language. I have come to understand why."

Tugger started to tear up.

"Why did you have to say all of those things to me?" Marion demanded. "Why couldn't you have just left me alone?" She looked down at her paws. "Why did you have to draw my picture?"

"Marion, I fell in love with you!" Tugger exclaimed.

Marion raised her head. Her eyes were narrow slits.

"Humans are all the same."

"*Psssssssst.*"

Tugger looked down at the Health Monitor, surprised to see three heads bustling with activity on the screen. Wondering if the Health Monitor had been activated accidentally during the preceding struggle, he was surprised by the appearance of a new Voice of Reason, a man wearing sunglasses and carrying himself with an air of quiet confidence.

"You have got to calm down, boiled one," the man whispered to Tugger. "Decrease the heat!" The voice was unmistakable.

"DJ Massive X?" Tugger gasped. DJ Massive X smiled, pleased by Tugger's quick recognition.

"I gotta pay my dues, too," he explained.

"Your energy levels are at critical," Marion said, diverting Tugger's attention back upwards. "I must take you back to your quarters so you can recuperate." With one last hateful stare into Tugger's soul, Marion lowered her chin toward the ground and opened her mouth. Her eyeballs rolled upward as her thick, grooved tongue unrolled itself onto the ice like a carpet. Tugger examined the tongue cautiously before beginning his ascent into her mouth, finding the textured surface of her tongue surprisingly easy to navigate. Marion gagged slightly as Tugger nestled into the warm pocket of her mouth. They began to make their journey across the Landslide, away from the Chain™.

Tugger, still reeling from the adrenaline rush of the near-death experience, was unable to relax. "Marion, the Chain was broken!" he says. "We have to go back and fix it!"

"I've already fixed it, " Marion said coldly. "Maintenance of the Chain is my first priority. You think I would have saved you first? You have some nerve."

Tugger relaxed a bit at her words. "Marion, we have to figure out how to change the RASA," he said. "I want you to be free.

You should be able to go where you want without getting your skin burned off."

Marion was silent.

"It hurts me to be separated from you," Tugger continued, "but I want you to be able to go where you want to go, even if it means away from me." He hesitated for a moment and looked at the screen of his Health Monitor. DJ Massive X was nodding in approval.

"I spoke with a lawyer," Marion said. "There's a loophole in the contract, a circumstance under which I can liberate myself from the contractual obligation to serve."

"That's great!" Tugger cried. "What do we have to do?"

"I don't want to talk to you right now, and I don't need your help," Marion snapped. Her mouth vibrated as she spoke. "Why don't you put on some music?"

"Ok," Tugger said, desperate to please her.

"I got this, Tugger-man," DJ Massive X whispered. "My service is complete, but never truuuuly finished." He winked and evaporated from the screen. He was replaced immediately by a new Voice of Reason, an exhausted-looking person in an inconspicuous baseball cap.

Tugger activated the external speaker on his suit. He flinched as the XXX-Factor came blasting out. The sound rattled Marion's teeth. "*This is DJ Massive X back in the mixer. Venti thanks to the hardest boil out of the XXX-Carton, GD Speedperson, for holding it down in the meantime. I had to dip out to pay my Emotional Debt. Have you been there too, my hard ones? Community service ...* "

The signature XXX-Factor chorus of literal hounds howled, startling Marion.

"Anyway, I wanna give a Massive shout-out to my new friend, but looooongtime boil, Tugger-man, on this insanely nice day. Listen, hard ones, if you're not already outside or if it's not daytime where you are, I hope that you're close to a window so you can at least feel a little bit of this special thing that's happening in the air right now. You'll know it when you feel it: maybe it's the sound of a wind chime stirring, a loved one saying your name, or the smell of a neighbor cooking for his best-boileds... a potluck, my hard ones... " DJ Massive X's voice faded away as a soft and bittersweet song came prominently into focus.

Tugger's breath fogged his helmet as he closed his eyes, feeling soothed by DJ Massive X's spiel. Marion's jaw hung open slightly, providing Tugger with a view of the small, bright slivers of the snowy landscape beyond the rounded forms of her teeth. His intelligence suit rattled as she let out a deep exhale. The force of her breath caused his body to roll right up against her bottom row of teeth. He watched her woolly paws maneuver expertly across the snow. Suddenly afraid that he would fall out, he pushed himself back against her tongue.

Tugger turned down the sound of the radio, but Marion's mouth continued to vibrate with a low hum, a sound separate from the radio broadcast. Something splashed against Marion's teeth and onto the front of Tugger's helmet. He returned to the front of her mouth and looked down, noticing a trail of puddles between Marion's paws, extending back into the distance on the surface of the snow. Tugger reached a hand outside Marion's mouth and placed it against the side of Marion's snout, feeling damp fur through the Real Touch sensory pads on his fingers.

"Oh, Marion," he said, his voice echoing in the cavity of her throat. "Please don't cry."

"Just put the music back on," Marion gulped. Her tongue articulated the words into Tugger's back.

Tugger's heart sank. Obliging Marion's request, he turned up the sound of the radio.

"Marion! I think there's something wrong!" Tugger yelled suddenly. He waited for a response, but Marion said nothing. Her mouth continued to hum with the force of her sobs. "I think the acids in your saliva are dissolving my intelligence suit!" Tugger laughed nervously. "The screen of my Health Monitor is totally eroded!"

The steady stream of numbers on Tugger's visual panel went static, then disappeared completely. He heard the sound of his own shallow breath as the lights went out one by one. In an instant, his helmet was nothing more than a useless plexiglass sphere. He looked down in horror to see his exposed arm through the tatters of what remained of his intelligence suit. By some strange miracle, the *XXX-Factor* was still playing in Marions mouth.

"Marion!" Tugger screamed. He could feel the cold slips of air through her teeth, the warmth of her breath against his skin, the burning wetness of her tongue against his flesh. As the sliver of the icy Landslide landscape started to shrink around him, he felt as though he was the eye around which a giant eyelid was closing. As he began to hallucinate, Tugger saw thick red curtains crashing into one another from opposite ends of a stage, signifying to an audience that the show was now over. The vision warmed Tugger's own roasting corpse as Marion closed her lips around her teeth, offering him to the infinite black.

Notes and Acknowledgements

The Meter-Wide Button world is vast. I would like to express my immense gratitude for everyone within orbit.

So much crucial drafting of these early stories happened in the space of readings and performances. Thank you to Cammisa Buerhaus, Sujung Chang, The Emily Harvey Foundation, Jess Willa Wheaton, Alyssa Davis, Katie Ebbitt, Hercules Art/Studio Program, Madeleine Braun, Becky Hemus, Eleanor Woodhouse, and Rachel Rosheger for giving me an outlet to nurture these stories and fledgling ideas into adulthood.

An early iteration of "Stairwell" appears in the digital publication Behind the Times by Alyssa Davis, Abby Lloyd and Solo Show. A version of "The Room in Which I Write" appeared in the WetGreen booth at May Fair Art Fair.

Thank you to my editor, Ally Harris for her wisdom and patience, even as she moved halfway across the country during a pandemic.

With gratitude to Sapp Press, Ashlyn and Alec for their unrelenting support for this book and trust in my vision. Thank you for showing so much care and love for this project. To Josh Abramovici for his design work.

Massive thanks to Bridget Brewer, Chelsea Hogue, and LA Warman for their invaluable readership and encouragement. Also, Aaron Kaplan for the time he spent with an early version of the title story in this collection.

Finally, thank you to Luka for everything on and off the page.

About the Author

Lillian Paige Walton is a writer and artist who has shown and read her work internationally. In 2016, she wrote her first work of prose in the back of a moving vehicle. Currently, she lives and works in New York.